"You saved my life."

Ashley reached forward and wrapped her hands around one of his. "In comparison to being killed, a broken leg is nothing."

He stared down at their joined hands, making her regret that she couldn't see his face. "It's not nothing," Dave said. "You don't know if you're going to be permanently handicapped. It's still scary."

She lowered her voice. "It hasn't been with you here. Thank you for all you've done."

Still not raising his head, he shifted his hands so now they covered hers. "It sounds like you're telling me you don't want me around anymore. If you are, I won't come back."

For some reason she didn't understand, her eyes started to burn. She wanted to rub it away, but she couldn't unless she pulled her hands out of his, and she didn't want to do that.

She gulped. "That's not what I'm saying at all. I'd like you to stay."

Dave raised his head and stared into her eyes. "I'd like that, too." He cleared his throat, released her hands, then stood.

Before she knew it, he was gone.

GAIL SATTLER,

an award-winning author of over forty books, lives in Vancouver, BC (where you don't have to shovel rain), with her husband, three sons, two dogs and a lizard who is quite cuddly for a reptile. Gail enjoys making music with a local jazz band and a community orchestra. When she's not writing or making music, Gail likes to sit back with a hot coffee and a good book.

GAIL SATTLER

The Best Man's Secret

HEARTSONG
PRESENTS

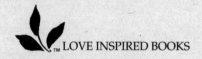 LOVE INSPIRED BOOKS

Recycling programs
for this product may
not exist in your area.

ISBN-13: 978-0-373-48718-9

THE BEST MAN'S SECRET

www.Harlequin.com

Printed in U.S.A.

Then you will know the truth,
and the truth will set you free.
—*John* 8:32

Dedicated to Tamela Hancock Murray, for too many reasons to write down. You are the best agent ever.

Chapter 1

Dave checked his watch as he pulled into the bank's last remaining parking spot. He didn't have the time to stop, but all he had was pocket change. He would never be caught unprepared without cash.

He didn't want to draw attention to himself, which he was about to do by walking into the bank wearing a tuxedo, but it couldn't be helped.

Giving himself a mental kick for his lack of planning, Dave sucked in a deep breath and slid out of the car. He hit the button twice to make sure the beep he heard was his own car, and jogged across the lot to the bank's main door.

As he reached forward to grasp the door handle, the clicking of heels echoed behind him. A blonde woman stepped through the door he pulled open, ahead of him. "Thanks," she muttered. "I'm kind of in a hurry."

"Yeah, I know the feeling. I'm kind of in a hurry, too."

Her cheeks turned an adorable shade of pink. "Sorry,"

she said, then she froze and scanned him from head to toe, taking in every inch of him, including the bow tie that suddenly seemed tighter and more uncomfortable. "Please, go ahead of me."

He couldn't help but tug at the bow tie, but it still felt like a noose around his neck. "Don't worry about it." One more person in front of him wasn't going to make any difference.

In unison, they both looked at the number of people waiting to use the ATM, then the lineup to the tellers.

"I think there are fewer people for the tellers," the woman said. "What do you think?"

"I agree. Only one ATM is working, and there are three tellers, so that line will probably go faster."

Side by side they hurried to the end of the line, which was only three people. His mother had always raised him to be a gentleman, so even though the clock was ticking he stepped aside and motioned for the woman to go ahead of him.

As if he had to justify to himself that he'd made the right decision, Dave turned to count the people at the ATM.

As he made eye contact with an elderly woman who was first in line there, she grinned from ear to ear, winked, then whistled at him. A number of women in the building turned their heads and stared at him.

Feeling the heat in his ears, he knew he was blushing. Worse than being embarrassed, though, he couldn't be the center of attention. To quickly put an end to it, he smiled widely at the elderly lady, and winked. She giggled, blew him a kiss, then stepped forward to use the ATM. When she continued her business, everyone else turned their attention back to what they were originally doing.

The line moved forward. The woman ahead of him

took the step, then turned around to face him. "You look like you're on your way to either a wedding or a fancy party."

Dave struggled not to check his watch. "A wedding."

"Yours?"

"No. I'm the best man." A wedding for himself was never going to happen. On days like today, that reality hit poignantly close to home.

Since he didn't elaborate, the woman once again turned to the front and stepped forward as the person at the front of the line moved to go to one of the tellers.

Within seconds two people at other tellers left at the same time, so the next person went to a teller, as well as the woman ahead of him, leaving him now first in line.

Automatically, Dave watched the man at the other teller, because that man would be done next, giving him his turn. The man slid a piece of paper to the teller, but instead of reaching into his back pocket for his wallet, the man's hand disappeared into his jacket pocket. The woman gasped and grasped the edge of the counter. Just like in the movies, metal flashed in the bright lights before Dave's brain registered what it was.

A gun.

"Back up!" the man shouted, waving the gun at the three tellers as he pressed what was obviously a phoney beard closer to his face with his free hand. Reaching into his jacket pocket, he then tossed a few bags onto the counter. The second his hand was free, he stepped sideways and grabbed the woman at the counter beside him— the woman Dave had entered with. The man yanked her arm, causing her to stumble. When she thumped against him he wrapped his hand around her neck and pointed the gun at her head. "Put everything from the tills into the bags, or she's dead! Everyone lay on the floor face down, hands above your heads. Everyone in the offices, get out here now, and get on the floor! Anyone makes one move for a cell phone, she's dead, and you'll be dead too."

Within seconds, everyone in the building was flat on the floor, including Dave. With his hands above his head, he turned his head sideways to watch and memorize details.

The teller's face paled. "We don't have a lot of money in the tills. All the big bills are in the vault."

"Shut up! Do as I say!" As the man yelled, he pressed the nozzle of the gun directly into his hostage's temple. "Fast! And don't be hitting no switches to call the cops."

Dave's heart pounded as he stared at the woman. He hadn't said more than a few words to her, but it was enough to have made a small connection. The gunman could never have planned in advance whom he would use as his prisoner, but he probably couldn't have picked anyone better, at least from a robber's perspective. The woman was small, both in stature and build. She looked on the thin side and below average height. To add to the image of fragility, she was blonde and fine-featured and wore shoes he didn't know how a human could walk in, much less run. Not that she could run, even if she were wearing track shoes. Her skirt narrowed at her knees, and would not only prevent her from running, he doubted if she could even take large steps. Her only defense would be to whack the gunman unconscious with her large purse. Except as the man pressed the gun to her head, she whimpered and dropped it, which left her empty-handed.

"Move it!" the man yelled, while at the same time he shook the woman, pressing the gun harder to her head. She gagged from the pressure of the hand around her neck, then winced as she gasped for air.

Dave knew what it was like to be on the wrong end

of a loaded gun. His heart pounded for the poor woman, who was, like he'd once been, simply in the wrong place at the wrong time.

Dave cleared his throat and raised his head, looking straight at the gunman, making sure his arms remained over his head with his palms flat on the floor. "Please. There isn't going to be enough money to make this worth the risk. Let her go. If you run out the door right now, you won't get caught."

The gunman glared at Dave, still pointing the gun at the terrified teller. "I won't get caught." He turned back to the teller. "Give me the bags. Now." He pressed the barrel of the gun against his hostage's head, rotating it back and forth, causing her eyes to widen. His voice lowered to a menacing drawl. "Now take the bags. Slowly."

Dave felt his own throat tighten. He prayed that nothing would go horribly wrong. That everyone would get out, no harm done, except for a little missing money.

The woman's face paled. With shaking arms, she reached forward and took the bags from the teller.

"If anyone moves, she gets it!" The robber lowered his voice. "We're going to walk to the door, you're going to kick the handicapped button with your foot, and—"

A flash of red and blue lights halted the gunman's words. He muttered a curse. By the way the woman stiffened, Dave could tell the man had tightened his grip around her neck. "You! Behind the counter! Turn out the lights! Fast!"

"I...I don't know where the switch is..." the teller choked out. "I'm...I'm new."

"Find it! Fast!"

"I know where the switches are. I'm the manager," a trembling voice drifted from behind a desk.

"You have ten seconds to kill the lights."

It took more than ten seconds for all the lights to go off, but nothing happened except it got darker in the building. With the lower level of light, the flash of the red and blue lights outside became more vivid, and more a reminder that the police were outside, no doubt with guns drawn.

From somewhere in the middle of the building came the sounds of a few women crying.

The blare of a man's voice from a bullhorn echoed through the plate glass windows. "We have your partner. The building is surrounded. Come out with your hands up and no one will get hurt."

"You! Pretty boy, stand up. Slowly, and keep your hands above your head."

For a few tense seconds silence hung in the air, until Dave realized that the gunman was speaking to him. As Dave stood, the man pulled a roll of duct tape out of his pocket and tossed in on the floor at Dave's feet, all the while keeping the gun on the woman's temple. "One at a time, tape everyone's hands together, and sit them over there, against the wall."

Dave knew better than to attempt to reason with the nervous man. At this critical time, the gunman would be scrambling for ideas for escape, which meant taking full control with no possibility that something unpredictable would happen. For now, Dave had no choice.

One at a time, counting everyone as he secured their hands then helped them to their feet to guide them to the inside wall, Dave did as he was told. When all were done, seventeen people sat against the wall with their hands taped together, in their laps. If he had to think of anything encouraging, the gunman hadn't said anything when he taped everyone's hands together in front of them rather than behind their backs. If this situation continued for very long, they wouldn't be as uncomfortable that way.

The man pushed his hostage forward. "Tape up his hands, then sit beside him. Don't try anything. If you do, I'll shoot someone. I have a lot of easy targets." He made a single sweep, pointing the gun in a wave at all the hostages now sitting lined up against the wall.

With the gun pointing to the back of her head, the woman took the roll of tape from Dave. When he held his hands forward toward her, he carefully bunched the fabric of the sleeves of the tux jacket between his wrists, and prayed that the man wouldn't notice that his wrists were not pressed tightly together. While he'd done his best to wrap everyone's wrists together loosely, he was the only hostage wearing a jacket on a summer day.

The woman's hands trembled as she carefully wound the tape around his wrists. As she did so, without moving her head, she looked into his eyes, as if apologizing for having to secure him. Even though she was probably terrified she held herself together, strong in the face of danger. It was a trait he admired, and something he'd tried to do himself with not as much success.

If his life were different, he would probably welcome the chance to get to know her better when this was over.

When she'd finished taping Dave's wrists together, the gunman wrapped her wrists with one hand, still holding the gun in his other. The second he was done, he pushed her roughly, causing her back to thump against the wall. "You get down, too," he barked.

The woman's eyes widened. "But..."

"Now!"

She stiffened, leaned back against the wall, pressed her bound hands to her skirt at her knees to hold it in place, pushed her knees together tightly, and started to sink. Just as her bottom hit the floor, the phone on the reception desk near the door rang.

Once again, he pointed the gun at her head. "What good timing." He looked up at the ceiling, obviously searching for the lenses of the hidden cameras. "Nobody move." Not taking his aim from the woman, he walked to the desk and picked up the phone. "No bargaining. I have hostages. I want a car and a plane going to Mexico. You have thirty minutes or I start shooting, one hostage at a time." Without waiting for a response, he hung up and walked back to the woman, holding the gun six inches from her forehead.

"You'd better hope they do it, because you're first." The gun wavered, then pointed at Dave's forehead. "Then, pretty boy, you're second."

Ashley stared at the gun, now pointing at the handsome man wearing the tuxedo. She should have felt relieved the gun was no longer aimed at her, but she didn't. Telling herself to breathe normally, she turned her head and looked at the man seated on the floor beside her.

It was like being on a movie set. A crazed gunman pointing a really big gun into the calm face of the handsome, brave, and impeccably dressed hero, staring the lunatic down with no fear in his deep brown eyes. In a split second, the handsome hero would lunge up, and in a feat of incredible strength and bravery, would disarm the evildoer. He'd turn him face down, step on his neck, and tie his hands behind his back. When the police stormed in with guns raised, there would be nothing to do except read the gunman his rights.

Except this hero's hands were tied, and he wasn't moving. Unlike James Bond, the man didn't appear to be ready to brandish a secret weapon to save the day. In fact, he couldn't reach into his pockets, even if he had a state-of-the-art stungun. With his hands secured together, he wouldn't even be able to bring himself to a standing position unless he was a martial arts expert. Somehow Ashley could imagine him being a martial arts expert.

In fact, dressed in the tux, he looked like James Bond. Sort of. Except younger. And more handsome. And his hair was medium brown and longer than the last James Bond she'd seen. And this man's tuxedo was probably rented. And he would probably lose his deposit.

All Ashley's thoughts dissolved back to reality as the gun turned back toward her.

"Now we wait," the gunman muttered, waving the gun in her face. "All of you sit still. I'm going to go over there, but my gun is pointed in the right direction." Before he'd even finished speaking, he backed up to the reception counter, the barrel of the weapon always pointed at someone in the row of hostages, dragged the chair out in front of it, and sat. He lowered his hand to his lap, but the gun remained firmly in his grip, ready to shoot, as threatened.

The man in the tuxedo turned to her, glanced down at her forearm, then returned his attention to her face. "Are you okay? You're doing really well, holding yourself together. You're doing great, actually."

Because he'd drawn her attention to it, Ashley looked down to see a purple bruise already appearing on her arm where the gunman had grabbed her. She raised her head and tried to smile, but she knew it looked as forced as it felt. "I'm okay, I guess." As okay as she could be, considering the circumstances, but she did appreciate his concern.

The trembling voice of an elderly lady sounded from the end of the row of people lined up on the floor. "I'm not okay. I have to use the ladies' room. I need my walker."

The gunman jumped to his feet and stared at the woman. Likewise, all heads turned. The gray-haired lady's wrinkled cheeks glistened with tears, and her lower lip was clenched between her teeth.

The woman who had said she was the manager spoke up. "I'll take her."

The man shook his head. "No." He pointed the gun back to the man in the tuxedo. "You. Pretty Boy. You take her." The gun pointed again at Ashley. "And if you think of trying anything funny, she's dead."

Ashley cleared her throat, trying to keep her voice steady as she spoke. "I don't understand."

The man in the tuxedo turned to her. "Someone who works here would probably know some way to open a back door. That's why he wants me to take her, and not a staff member."

The gunman's eyes narrowed, he stared at the man in the tuxedo, and stiffened. "Do you work here?"

The man shook his head. "No."

"How do you know about a back door?"

"I watch a lot of movies."

"Then you'll know I'm serious, and unlike in the movies, once I start shooting, no one gets out of here alive. No funny stuff. You've got three minutes." In a swift motion, he grabbed Ashley's hair, bringing the sting of tears to her eyes, and pressed the barrel of the gun to her temple. "Or else."

The man nodded. Using his bound hands, he awkwardly pushed himself to his feet.

Once standing, he walked to the elderly lady and helped her stand. "I'll be as fast as I can." The woman held on to his arm to steady herself, and the two of them walked to where the bank employee directed them.

The entire time they were gone, the nose of the gun

remained pressed against Ashley's skin, making it feel like it would leave a permanent circle. Only when the man and elderly lady returned did he withdraw it. The man assisted the lady to sit on the floor, then returned to his own designated holding spot. He leaned his back against the wall and slid down until he was again seated on the floor.

The robber returned to the chair, scowled, and checked his watch. At his unpleasant expression, Ashley prayed the police were indeed doing as the madman had ordered—securing a car and a private plane to Mexico. All she knew was she'd never been so scared in her entire life. As she looked up at the clock on the wall, the second hand moving so slowly, she calculated that it had only been twelve minutes, yet the tension had risen exponentially with every rotation of the second hand, ticking around its circle.

The ringing of the phone on the desk caused everyone to flinch, including the robber. He scooped it up. "What!" he hollered. "This better be good news." His scowl deepened as he listened, then he rammed the phone down with a slam and began to pace.

"This doesn't look good," she murmured to the man in the tuxedo.

"We don't know that. It could be just a small delay and he's overreacting. Which isn't good, but it's not necessarily bad. By the way, my name's Dave."

She turned to him. "I'm Ashley." She lowered her voice to a bare whisper. "You seem so calm, are you a cop or something?"

Dave shook his head. "I wish I was, but no."

She waited for him to say what he did do for a living, but this really wasn't the time nor the place for small talk, or any talk, as much as she would have welcomed the distraction. But at the same time, she noticed him wiggling his hands every time the gunman wasn't looking. She hadn't bound his hands all that tight, plus she had wrapped the tape on the outside of his sleeves. If he managed to work his hands free, she wondered what he thought he could do against an agitated man with a gun. But she was too afraid to ask him. She turned and looked into his eyes, hoping her expression would convey her question, even if he couldn't give her a verbal answer.

Without moving his head his eyes turned quickly toward the gunman, then he shook his head.

At least he understood part of the question. The answer she got from him was that he was indeed trying to free his hands, but not going to do anything about it, at least not yet.

The robber turned to them. All Dave's motions stopped. The man glared at Ashley. Her insides turned to ice. "They said they're almost ready. When the car is here and the plane is standing by, you're coming with me."

Ashley shook her head. "No. Please. Don't make me go."

He grinned a feral grin. "You're my plane ticket, missy. When we land in Mexico, then we'll go our separate ways."

Ashley didn't see that happening. What she could see was that he'd shoot her—and the pilot. Then he'd sell the plane to a Mexican drug cartel and live happily ever after with all the money from the plane and the robbery, without guilt, for the rest of his life.

Her stomach lurched at the thought of her own death. While she knew she would see her Lord in Heaven, she wasn't ready to go there quite yet. She hadn't met her soul mate, the love of her life. She hadn't had children. She hadn't seen the aurora borealis, and she'd only watched *It's a Wonderful Life* once.

"No…" She whimpered. "Please. Don't make me go. I'll give you anything. Please don't take me with you."

The phone rang again. The man listened for two seconds and hung up. "It's time. Stand up. We're going."

Chapter 2

Dave watched Ashley's face pale to a chalky white while she turned over on all fours, or was that threes, with her hands taped together? She wobbled awkwardly as she pushed herself to her feet, then once standing, flattened her back against the wall. While the robber's attention remained fixed on her, Dave again frantically wiggled his wrists, trying to pull one hand out. Once they left the building Ashley's hours of life were numbered at the hands of a desperate man. The robber would force Dave to drive the car while he held Ashley at gunpoint, then leave Dave behind when he got on the plane, still using Ashley as a hostage to force the pilot to do his bidding. Once they landed, her usefulness would be over and she'd turn into a liability. The man would then either kill her, or abandon her in a place where she'd probably be killed, or worse, by someone else.

He couldn't let that happen.

With the metal buttons on the cuffs of the tuxedo jacket digging into his wrists, he worked frantically to free his hands. Slowly, the pressure against his wrists loosened as he worked the buttons to rest on the sides of his hands. Pressing his wrists together once more, he pulled and wiggled. With a rush of blood as one of the buttons bit through his skin, one hand became free. Before anyone could notice, he slipped his now-free hand below the loose sleeve.

"Everyone!" the gunman yelled. "Push away from the counter and lay face down, hands above your heads." He turned the gun back to Dave. "You, Pretty Boy, don't move."

Dave looked up at Ashley, the barrel of the gun inches from her head. "Whatever you say."

"Good." As the robber moved the gun to point at the far end of the line of people, each person followed his commands. While his attention remained fixed on the elderly lady, who was slower than everyone else at stretching out on the floor, Dave looked up at Ashley. Fortunately she looked back at him, so he subtly showed her that his hands were free. He made the numbers one, two, then three with his fingers, then lowered his head slightly. She gave him a small nod back, so he hoped she understood what he was trying to tell her.

When the elderly lady was finally stretched out on the floor, the gunman turned and pointed the gun back to Dave. "Stand up. Walk ahead of me and be my shield. You," he pointed the gun at Ashley, "I'm going to keep you right here, right next to me. When we get outside, stop, or I shoot her. I want them to bring the car to the door so there's no chance anyone can get behind and shoot me. Then you're both getting in the car. You, Pretty

Boy, you're driving, and she stays in the back seat with me. Get it?"

"Yes." Dave's heart began to pound. It was starting. He told himself not to panic. For now, no one would get hurt if everyone did as the gunman said. But if the man noticed Dave's hands were no longer bound, that would start a chain of events from which there would be no turning back.

"Stand."

He didn't know how he was going to obey and not show his unrestrained hands. But just as he started to move, Ashley crouched and coughed. The gunman moved downward with her, keeping the gun pointed at her head, watching to keep the gun where he wanted it, against her temple. With the man bent, Dave quickly stood, repositioning his now-free hand beneath the tape before the gunman looked back, so it would like he was still secured.

Surprise registered on the gunman's face when he turned and saw Dave already standing. "Okay, Pretty Boy. Get in front of me, then walk real slow to the door."

Dave's mind raced. Facing forward, in front of Ashley and the gunman, he wouldn't be able to show Ashley when to duck if she couldn't see his hands. But he had to do as he was told. Now standing, Dave studied heights and positions—the man held the gun with his right hand to Ashley's right temple, Ashley's head at the man's left shoulder.

He stepped in front of them, and they shuffled toward the door.

They were out of time. Once outside, surrounded by police and guns pointing, every nerve would be on edge, lessening the chance for his plan, as unplanned as it was, to work. Dave cleared his throat. "There's two doors.

I don't know which one..." He emphasized the word "one," then counted in his head. Two. Three. The gunman cursed, which hopefully meant Ashley had ducked.

He'd worked to get his brown belt in Tai Kwan Do with self-defense in mind, but never thought he'd need it for something like this. Everything he'd done had been at the dojo with padded mats and helpful sparring partners. But it was now or never, and never wasn't an option. Technically, he could do this.

In split-second timing, Dave spun and grabbed the gunman's right wrist with his left hand. Just like at sparring practice, he twisted the man's arm upward and back so the gun pointed to the ceiling. As the gunman stiffened with the shock, Dave grabbed the man's elbow with his right hand, twisted it sharply, and pushed upward. If the gunman didn't arch backward and rebalance his weight, this move would break his arm. Even if his arm didn't break, Dave knew the pain associated with this maneuver.

Balancing all his weight on his left foot, Dave hooked his right leg around the man's right leg, behind the knee. At the same time as Dave pushed the man's elbow up with his palm, he used his right leg to knock the man off balance, causing them both to go down in a controlled fall. Always remaining on top, Dave never released his grip on the gunman's wrist, keeping his leg wound around the gunman's.

As they hit the floor together, with Dave's weight on top, the man's breath rushed out of him on impact. Almost in parallel motion, beside them, Ashley also toppled to the floor. She rolled to her stomach, then began to push herself up.

The man's wrist tightened, making Dave aware that he had managed to keep his grip on the gun. Now that they were both on the floor, the gun was no longer pointed safely at the ceiling.

Dave's heart raced as the man's wrist continued to tighten. Using all his strength, he pulled the gunman's wrist upward, then smashed it down to the floor. The gun remained in the man's hand. Dave didn't know exactly where it was pointing, but nowhere was good right now. Tightening his grip even more, Dave steeled his strength to repeat the move, but before he could pull the man's hand upward, his wrist tightened. Dave's arm jerked with the ricochet of the recoil from the explosive release of the gunshot.

Dave froze. Ashley had started to run away, but suddenly she lurched, then fell. A bright red stain marred Ashley's skirt, growing larger and larger.

Beneath Dave's grip, the man once again began to struggle. A strength Dave had never known empowered him. He raised the man's hand and again smashed it to the hard tile floor. This time the gun flew out of the man's hand. As soon as it started to slide across the cold floor, the hostages all scrambled to their feet and ran for the door.

The second the door opened, a number of officers ran in with guns raised. One of them barked into a radio. "Need medics, stat. Shots fired. Civilian down."

In a blur of motion, two officers stood above him with guns raised. As soon as the officer finished reciting the Miranda Rights, Dave released his grip and rolled off for them to cuff the man and drag him to his feet. In the tussle, the robber's fake beard, glasses, and hat had come off, revealing the clean-cut face of a young man who should have been going to college, not robbing a bank. But experience had taught Dave that faces such as these were the most deceptive. In general, people didn't expect such an innocent face to have evil behind it.

As they led the young man out the door, instead of following, Dave remained seated on the cold floor watching helplessly while the medics attended to Ashley.

This was his fault.

His throat tightened as he watched her respond to their prompts and questions. When she began to complain he thought that was probably the best sign possible. Even though the bleeding was severe, the attendants remained calm as they controlled the gunshot wound to prepare her for transport to the nearest hospital.

Outside, since the police had appeared with the bad guy adequately restrained, the buzz from the crowd escalated from the white noise of hundreds of hushed conversations to a dull roar, accented by officers using bullhorns in an attempt to disperse the crowd. This only fired up the reporters, who weren't leaving without a story.

Dave knew what the turn of events would be. Outside, no one as of yet knew what had occurred inside the bank's doors. So far, only the hostages and five of the dozen or so police officers in attendance knew what had happened, and what he'd done.

But soon everyone would. Especially the news media. It would be on the internet in minutes, complete with pictures.

Word of what happened would spread quickly, and within seconds of his walking out the door, countless cameras and cellphones would be taking photos of him. His name and photo would not only be splashed all over every newspaper in the country, he'd be in vivid color on the blogs of everyone in attendance, and every step would soon be posted on YouTube.

He couldn't let that happen.

Outside, the police worked to control the crowd. Once they were satisfied, they would move all the hostages to a secure location to give their reports. They'd probably also send everyone, including himself, for trauma counseling. Dave wouldn't do that. He'd already had enough counseling to last more than a lifetime.

His report wouldn't matter. Nothing he would say would matter. There were enough witnesses, and the bad guy had been caught. All his actions were on the bank's video if there were any doubt of anyone's testimony. It was time for him to leave.

Dave stood and moved farther away as the medics moved Ashley onto a stretcher, lifted her onto the gurney, checked to make sure she was stable, and began pushing her to the ambulance waiting outside the bank's door.

Through the smoked glass window, red lights flashed. The second the back door of the ambulance opened the crowd began to shuffle from the area close to the bank's door to the ambulance, no doubt wanting to take pictures of the latest victim of a gunshot that should never have been fired.

He was the only one left in the building as the crowd focused all their attention on Ashley and the attendants made their way to the ambulance.

Before anyone came looking for him, Dave slipped off the tuxedo jacket and then his shirt, leaving him only in his undershirt and the pants. Not his usual style of dress, but no one had been looking at his face. Everyone would only remember him as the guy in the tuxedo. On the floor near his feet lay the gunman's fake beard and baseball cap. Even though it was evidence, Dave picked up the hat, slipped it on, then fished through the tuxedo jacket's pockets for his sunglasses, and put them on. He bundled the jacket and shirt into a ball under his arm, and like Elvis, left the building as unobtrusively as he could. A few people noticed him, but most attention was focused on Ashley as the attendants prepared to move her into the back of the ambulance. People looked past him, no doubt waiting for the guy in the tuxedo, not a slob wearing a sleeveless undershirt and a beat-up baseball cap.

Dave eased into the crowd, blending in with the rest of the gawkers. As he thought would happen, a police officer with a reporter not far behind started walking toward the building, probably looking for the guy in the tuxedo. As the officer continued inside, Dave turned and made his way to the rear of the crowd, struggling not to appear like he was rushing. As soon as he got to the parking lot he couldn't help himself, and ran the rest of the way to his car.

He didn't know Ashley's last name, but he would find out somehow. It was his fault that she'd been shot. He hadn't thought ahead to the possibility that the man would be able to hold on to the gun. His error in judgment made it his responsibility to help her until she was healed. No small injury—a gunshot wound in the leg would take a long time to heal. Then she'd have the physical therapy and recuperation period. Or, if this became a worst case scenario, the possibility existed that she would never be able to walk again.

Because this was his fault, it was his duty to assist her until she could get back to her normal life—unlike himself. He would never have a normal life, so he would make sure that her life could go on as normally as possible when this was all over.

He started the engine and exited the parking lot. For now, he had a wedding to go to. But like Arnie, he'd be back.

"Ready to go?"

Lying flat on her back, Ashley looked up at the medic, his face framed by the white ceiling of the ambulance.

She tried to nod, but with her head secured, she couldn't. She didn't know why they'd done that. There was nothing wrong with her neck. She'd been shot in the leg. Yet she was immobilized from head to toe.

Panic began to gnaw at her. "I don't know," she muttered, trying to sound more confident than she felt.

"Don't worry," the attendant said as he smiled. She imagined it was the same smile he would give a terrified child. "You're going to be fine." He turned his head. "We're ready," he called to the driver. Through the narrow window at the top of the ambulance walls, the red light flashed. The siren started to wail, and the vehicle began to move forward.

"You say that to everyone, don't you? I don't think I'm going to die, at least not today, but is there something I don't know? Something you can't tell me?"

He patted her shoulder. "We're not allowed to give any diagnosis or prognosis, but off the record I can tell you that you'll be fine. You didn't lose that much blood, and after they remove the bullet, after the PT, your life will be pretty much back to normal. The worst that will happen is you won't be able to compete in the Olympics."

Ashley tried to wiggle her toes. She couldn't feel them on her right foot. In fact, she couldn't feel her whole right leg.

She struggled to breathe. "What do you mean remove the bullet?" She didn't want surgery. Now she knew that she was hurt worse than she thought.

"There is no exit wound. That's a good thing for now because that doesn't bleed so much. We'll be at the hospital soon. You have a good medical plan, don't you?"

She did, but she didn't know if it covered being shot. It was a possibility she'd never considered. "I've never been in the hospital before."

He patted her hand and smiled. "Don't worry. The food isn't as bad as all the jokes. Not nearly as bad, anyway."

She noticed he hadn't said anything about surgery or pain or recovery, but that was probably because he was trying to keep her calm. She would do that. She would stay calm.

The attendant patted her hand again. "All you have to do is get your boyfriend to sneak in some snacks or a burger after a few days. Or maybe a husband? I see you're not wearing a ring, but not everyone wears a ring anymore."

Automatically, Ashley tried to shake her head, only to be reminded the hard way that she couldn't move. "No. No husband." No boyfriend either. But she would have many visits from her twin brother, the only family she had left.

She squeezed her eyes shut. Right now Evan had enough to do without worrying about her, even though he would come to visit when he could. She would probably see more of Natasha, her best friend. But Natasha wouldn't sneak in ordinary food. Natasha would sneak in Chunky Monkey, not only for the two of them, but probably also for some of the nurses.

Once she was out of surgery and in a normal room…

Ashley squeezed her eyes shut to block out thoughts of surgery. The only medical procedure she'd ever had was at a local clinic, getting a few stitches after she'd fallen off her bike as a child. But she'd heard a few horror stories from some of the other teachers at her school.

Each bump and change in speed of the ambulance as it rushed her to the hospital reminded Ashley of her upcoming surgery. Instead of thinking of being put under anesthetic and the surgeon's blade she tried to focus on something else. But all she could see in her mind was the robbery, like a feed on YouTube repeating over and over—including the fear and the pain of getting shot. Rather than focus on the bad things, Ashley turned her thoughts to the one good thing—Dave.

He'd saved her life. Once they landed in Mexico the robber wouldn't have needed her anymore, and it would have been more expedient to kill her than to send her back home safely.

In saving her, Dave could have been killed, but instead he'd risked his life and defeated the robber just like the martial arts expert she'd imagined he could be.

Just like James Bond. Only this hero was real. And he didn't have any fancy gadgets.

She couldn't help but wonder if he made it to his friend's wedding on time, and if he was thinking of her as she was thinking of him.

Dave wiggled the bow tie that threatened to choke him and forced his concentration back to Tyler and Brittany. With stars in their eyes and holding hands they recited their vows, proclaiming love and commitment to each other in front of their friends, their families, their pastor, and God.

At the high point of the entire ceremony, all Dave could think of was the face of a stranger as the paramedics loaded Ashley onto the gurney.

Today had been life-changing for her. After she healed physically, her perspective would change. She'd always be watching around herself, wondering if someone who appeared normal had a hidden agenda.

Hopefully the investigation would determine that the robbery was simply the desperate actions of a couple of losers. If so the courts would determine that her life would go on pretty much as normal, even though it wouldn't be that simple.

He didn't know if Ashley would be offered trauma counseling, but he doubted it. In the eyes of the law this would probably be considered a simple robbery gone bad, but for anyone who spent even a second at the wrong end of a gun, it wasn't so easy to trust the world again.

He wondered if she'd ever been on the right end of a gun. Somehow he doubted it.

Even though he hadn't been the one holding the gun, Ashley's getting shot was his fault. In addition to a long recovery for her physical injuries there would be significant mental trauma that could go on for years.

He didn't know if she had someone to look after her.

When he'd secured everyone's hands during the robbery he'd noticed Ashley hadn't been wearing any rings. If she were truly single and lived alone, when the nightmares happened she would wake up screaming into an empty house.

He shook himself out of those thoughts as Tyler and Brittany exchanged their rings and Pastor Rob pronounced them man and wife.

His best friend was now a married man. If necessary, Tyler would lay down his life for his wife, and one day, his children.

Dave's throat tightened. He would never be a married man. He carried too much baggage. He didn't have just a suitcase—his baggage filled an entire truck.

He needed to make certain that Ashley wouldn't have to carry the same baggage as he did. After the ceremony, and after the photos he agreed to do, he knew where he was going.

Chapter 3

The world spun as Ashley opened her eyes. To quell the rolling motion in her stomach she squeezed them shut, then reopened one eye. Slowly. The world remained blurry.

"You're awake," a smooth male voice drifted into her consciousness. "Aside from the obvious, how are you, sweetie?"

Ashley opened both eyes, seeking the owner of the voice. Even though she shouldn't have been able to move her head, she did. Of course. She wasn't in the ambulance anymore. She'd had the surgery and obviously lived through it.

She forced the strange man's face into focus. She should know him, especially since he'd called her by an endearment, but her brain wasn't working properly yet.

He leaned toward her, picked up her hand in his, gave it a gentle squeeze and leaned down, as if he was going to kiss her cheek. But instead of making contact, he whispered in her ear. "I had to tell them that I was your boyfriend. It was pretty hard when I don't know your last name. If you don't remember me, I'm Dave. Dave Ducharme."

The memories of the bank robbery, being used as a hostage then saved by her rescuer melded into a scene that should have been from a movie, except it was real because here she was in the hospital. She'd just had surgery to remove a bullet from her leg because she'd been shot.

She opened her mouth to respond, but the dryness was almost overwhelming.

Dave straightened and patted her hand. "Don't try to talk. You're going to be okay. The surgeon says everything went well and you'll be up and about in no time."

She couldn't help it. Tears began to well up in her eyes, and they started to burn. She cleared her throat as best she could. "Am I really going to be okay? Or are they just saying that?" Come to think of it, she'd never heard anyone actually say she was going to be fine except for the medic in the ambulance, and it was probably his job to say that to everyone.

Dave gave her hand a gentle squeeze. "Yes. The doctor told me what they had to do, and what we're going to need to do to get you mobile again. I won't say it's not bad, but it could have been a lot worse. Everything is going to be okay now. It's just a matter of time."

As her head cleared a little more, she focused all her attention on Dave's eyes. Everything about his expression told her he was being sincere. Except he didn't quite say the words she wanted to hear. He'd said it was just a matter of time, but until what? He didn't say that it would just be a matter of time and she'd be skiing, even if she'd never skied before.

He patted her hand again. "I can see it in your eyes. Don't worry. You're going to be fine."

She continued to look at him, taking in the whole picture that her limited range of vision could allow without moving her head too much. She was now very aware from the scratchy feeling that she had a tube up her nose.

Dave was wearing a white shirt with the top buttons undone.

He squeezed her hand a little tighter. "Is there anyone you'd like me to call? No one knows where your purse is. They're probably holding it as evidence or maybe it's still on bank's floor, so I couldn't use your cell phone." He motioned his head to a nearby nurse who was making no effort to hide that she was listening to their conversation. "I don't have your family's numbers memorized. You know how it is with everyone on speed dial."

"What time is it? How long have you been here?"

He smiled, and his deep brown eyes crinkled at the corners. "I stayed at Tyler and Brittany's wedding only as long as I had to. Everyone was asking about you of course, so as soon as the ceremony was over I rushed here so I could be with you when you woke up."

She supposed she needed to pretend not only that she knew who Tyler and Brittany were, but that she also should have been at the wedding.

He turned his head and looked directly at the nurse, who was reading the chart of the patient in the next bed. "Excuse me? Nurse, would you mind getting me a pen and paper so I can write down everyone's phone numbers?"

The nurse smiled. "Sure. I'll be right back."

The second the nurse was out of potential hearing range, Dave leaned closer to Ashley, speaking barely above a whisper. "Who should I call? I hope you're not married. If you are that could get really awkward really fast."

"No, not married. No boyfriend." She tried to smile, which reminded her of the tube up her nose. "My last name is Kruger. My brother's name is Evan, his wife's name is Karen. No parents, no other family. My best friend is Natasha. We'd just been out for lunch, we were both going to go home to change, then meet up with some other friends at the park. Maybe she thinks I changed my mind and stood her up, but she's probably worried about me because I said I'd call when I was ready to go, and I didn't. I'd like you to call her."

He lowered his voice even more. "Please tell me that you have a job with a medical plan. The staff asked about your coverage, and I told them you were good."

"Yes, I do."

Before she could tell him anything else a boyfriend would know, the nurse arrived with a pen and paper.

Dave flattened the paper on his knee and poised the pen to write. "What's Evan and Karen's number? I should probably call Natasha, too." As soon as she gave him the numbers, before she had a chance to thank him for calling everyone for her, the nurse stepped between them and looked up at Dave. "You have to go now. She needs to rest, and then when the surgeon says it's okay, we'll move her to a ward. You can come back during visiting hours."

Dave stood, pocketed the paper, and held out the pen for the nurse. "I understand. I'll be back later."

Before Ashley could tell him that wouldn't be necessary, he reached for her right hand, the one that didn't have the IV attached, and pressed a soft kiss to the back of her hand. "See you later, sweetie," he whispered in a low drawl, then turned and walked away.

The nurse's eyes followed him out of the doorway. "He looks like a keeper," she said with a smile as he left.

Ashley bit her lower lip. She had no intention of finding out if he was a keeper. When he came back to talk to her once she was out of the post-surgical unit with no nurses in hearing range she could thank him properly for everything, and she'd never see him again. In a way that was a shame, but that was the way it had to be.

Dave stood back while Evan gave his sister a cautious hug, being careful not to disturb all the wires and tubes connected to her.

By meeting Ashley's brother, Dave learned a lot about Ashley. First, he'd found out a few things a boyfriend should know—that she was an elementary school teacher, and she did indeed have a good medical plan. He'd also learned that Ashley and Evan were twins. Of course, being opposite gender they couldn't be identical twins, but there was no doubt the two of them were related. Both blond, both thin, and they both had the same blue eyes and fair complexion.

As well, Evan was the proud new father of twins. Though Evan had insisted he would take care of Ashley, it wasn't possible. Evan's wife and new daughters had only been home for two days, and already Evan had dark circles under his eyes. Having to take care of his sister in addition to his wife and two children while carrying on at his job, would soon drive Evan to the point of exhaustion. Besides, Ashley wouldn't get the rest she needed being in the same house as two newborn babies.

Before Dave had arrived at Ashley's brother's home he'd phoned Natasha, Ashley's best friend. Natasha couldn't look after Ashley either, because she had to leave Monday morning for an extended business trip.

However, Ashley and Evan were very involved in their church community. Many families would be able to bring meals and check on her on a regular basis. More than the help, this piece of information told Dave that Ashley was a believer, which was very good. This was a time in her life she needed to lean on God and trust that God would take care of her.

Dave sucked in a deep breath as he considered the ramifications. When God helped in Biblical days He often sent angels, but in modern times it didn't work like that. In today's world, God sent people.

The very moment Dave realized Ashley had been shot and that he had brought it about through negligence, Dave had promised himself, and God, that he would do all he could to help her while she recovered.

Little did he realize at the time what that would entail.

As Dave watched, Evan pulled his cell phone out of his pocket, turned off the WiFi, then proudly displayed the latest photos of his new daughters. As Ashley oohed and aahed over the photos, Evan yawned. Then, seeing Evan yawn, so did Ashley.

Dave stepped forward. "I think she needs to rest, and so do you."

They both nodded, even though he didn't need confirmation.

Dave motioned to the bag of clothes they'd brought from Ashley's apartment. "We brought you some stuff."

Ashley's face paled. "What do you mean? Were you at my place? It's a mess."

Dave shrugged his shoulders. "It's not that bad. It just looks like you left in a rush. I've seen worse." She didn't know it, but he and Evan had talked about Dave keeping the key, at least for a few days, so he could help get her apartment ready for her to come home. Evan was both exhausted and busy, but Dave had nothing better to do.

They'd come in one car to save on the cost of parking, and that also gave them time to talk without crying babies in the background. Then, as soon as Dave took Evan home, he would return to Ashley's abode to clean up, then rearrange her cupboards and counters to make everything she needed easily accessible. Dave knew what it was like to depend on crutches, and it wasn't as easy as most people thought. Fortunately her apartment building had an elevator so she didn't need to use the stairs for access to her second-floor suite.

Later, when Evan's wife and both babies were asleep, Evan would return to Ashley's apartment and he and Dave would start rearranging the furniture.

While they'd talked, Evan had made a good suggestion, so another thing Dave needed to do was talk to the building superintendent.

"Come on, Evan, I'll take you home." He looked toward Ashley. "I'll be back in the morning after church. See you tomorrow."

Ashley leaned against the door frame while taking in her apartment. Or, what used to be her apartment. It was her furniture and the walls were the same color, but aside from that, she barely recognized the place. If she hadn't been watching out the window for the entire ride in the car, she would have doubted they'd arrived at the right building.

"What have you two done?"

Behind her, Dave cleared his throat. "Nothing much. We just made it easier for you to get around and reach your things."

She wished she could point, but she feared if she let

go of the crutches, she'd fall. "The only thing in the same place, besides the pictures on the walls, is my television." Everything else, even the couch, was spread around the room so that nothing was against the walls.

"Evan wanted to move everything around so you would always have something to lean on. Now you won't have to use the crutches every time you have to move around your apartment. We fixed up the bathroom and your bedroom, too."

Ever since they lost their parents, Evan had gone over the top to help when he thought she needed it. This would have been fine if it were just Evan getting some mutual friends to help, but that he'd taken advantage of Dave, just because he was there, wasn't right. They had no right to ask so much of him.

"Thank you. But I'll be okay. Many of the ladies from my church will help me. I'm pretty sure they'll bring meals and even do some of my housekeeping until I'm on my feet."

"Evan said the same thing. But he also told me that it's not realistic to expect that someone will be here every time you need something. And what if you fall?"

She could imagine everything Evan had said. He'd been reading too many books about all the things that could go wrong with babies, and since she'd ganged up with Karen to get him to stop, he'd apparently transferred all his fears to her situation.

However, Evan was right. Regardless of Evan's paranoia, despite promises made while she was in the hospital and the best of intentions, everyone had busy lives. For a week or maybe two, she would be well cared for while confined to the couch all day. Then, as time went on the urgency would fade. Even though she would still need help after the cast came off, by then, in people's minds, she would be all better. The doctor had warned her that because a gunshot had caused the break, the bone wasn't merely broken; it had been shattered. It would take longer to heal, and she had to be very careful not to put stress on it, especially in the early stages. Short of hiring a day-nurse, which she couldn't afford, she was going to be very alone most of the time. "I know you and Evan worked very hard. Rearranging my furniture like this will really help. Thank you very much."

"There's also something you should know."

The way Dave's voice dropped when he spoke told her this was something she wasn't going to like. Before she bit his head off, she reminded herself that Dave was only the messenger. Evan, smart man that he was, had abandoned Dave to take all the heat for what he'd done. She turned to watch Dave as he spoke, but the second she looked at him, he turned away, looking at the television, the curtains, the entrance to the kitchen—anywhere but at her.

Finally he turned his head so their eyes met. "You have a new neighbor upstairs."

Ashley thought back to the two young men who had previously lived above her. With only eight suites in the building all the residents passed each other often. The two young men from the upper floor had been polite and easy to talk to when she met them in the elevator, but it hadn't been good living below them. She didn't know what they did for a living, but every evening the television blared from dinner time until nearly 2:00 a.m. They didn't have wild parties on the weekends, so her complaints to the landlord had gone without resolution. She was the only one disturbed by the noise, which wasn't extreme to anyone but her, living below them. They had two televisions going at the same time, one in the bedroom above hers, and the other in the living room, which was above her own living room. At the same time they both watched different programs, sounding like they were trying to drown each other out.

They'd moved out three months ago, and it had been close to paradise with no noise coming through the ceiling.

"Have a couple of rowdies moved in?" Ashley paused to listen, trying to hear something from above, but there was only silence.

Dave cleared his throat. "Evan doesn't want you to be all alone. Don't be mad at him, because I really don't mind. He wants you to be close to someone who can help you when you need it, but everyone you both know lives at least half an hour away. So he asked if I could move in upstairs for a while so you'd have someone close by when you need help."

Chapter 4

Dave stiffened and tried to smile.

Ashley stared up at him. A lesser man would have melted in the heat of her glare. "Excuse me?"

"I really don't mind. I want to help." More than anything, he knew what it was like to be down for the count and alone, and the guilt was eating him. He didn't want Ashley to suffer through that, although she wouldn't be as alone as he had been. At first Evan had been hesitant about Dave living in the same building, but in the last week they'd come to know each other a bit better. More important, Dave knew Evan had been very diligent on checking up on him.

"Evan had no right to ask that of you."

She was wrong. Evan did have the right because Dave was the cause of her injury, and they all knew it. "Actually, he did. It's my fault you were shot, so this is the least I can do. He said that you don't really know any of your neighbors, and even if you did, he said they're not home very much. If you hurt yourself and were screaming at the top of your lungs for help, no one would come. That's not right."

Ashley's eyes narrowed and her lips tightened.

Dave tried not to gulp. Things had gotten more than a little awkward, but he couldn't *not* do this. If he hadn't felt bad enough, after talking with Evan over the last few days, the guilt was now eating him up. If she got hurt, or worse, some sicko took advantage of her when she couldn't defend herself, then that, too, would be his fault. He couldn't live with something worse happening to her. And he hadn't needed Evan to remind him of that, either. He already felt that way before all Evan's comments.

Finally he managed to force a smile. "People from the church can't be here every time you need help, but I can. All you have to do is call or text me, and I can be here in about a minute, day or night, depending how long I have to wait for the elevator." Or thirty-seven seconds if he ran down the stairs.

She dragged one hand down her face. "I really can't ask that of you. I'm sure you don't want to leave your own home."

"It's okay. I've decided to sublet it for a while." Which was no loss. He kept a minimum of personal things in his apartment. Everything he truly valued he could put in one box, which was currently now in the suite above him with the rest of what he would need during the next few months.

"What about your job?"

He shrugged. "I've made arrangements with my boss to work from home for a while. I often do that anyway. I'll only need to go to the office to pick up and deliver projects when I'm done. I work for an accounting firm.

This time of year, when personal income tax season is over we do the business taxes and profit and loss statements. My boss actually prefers us to work at home for the corporate accounts because then he doesn't have to pay for coffee. He's a great boss, but sometimes he can be a bit of a tightwad. So my days and hours are flexible."

Her eyes widened as she stared at him. "Are you sure about this?"

Dave spread his arms, palms upward. "This is the slowest time of the year for me at work. In fact, I'm due for some vacation time. This seems like a good time to take it."

All she did was stare at him.

Dave cleared his throat. "You really shouldn't be standing. You should be sitting on the couch. I know crutches are hard on your armpits. Let's get you settled, and we can talk more. Would you like some coffee? I bought real cream. I hate that powdered stuff. Did you know it's not powdered milk, it's oil based?"

"Have you and Evan cleared out my fridge, too? Why are you doing this?"

Dave could hear the suspicion in her tone. He ran his fingers through his hair. "Evan was concerned about your perishables with you gone. Your brother's a little overprotective, isn't he?"

"Unfortunately, yes. For years we only had each other, and now, of course, he has his wife and daughters. He's been used to looking after me for a long time. So he does tend to worry about me too much."

"Anyway, he was tired, so I finished organizing, then I threw out all the stuff that was questionable and did some grocery shopping for you."

She just looked at him in as if she were sizing him up. "I don't even know you. You could be an ax murderer."

"Evan is thorough. He called my pastor, boss, and landlord for references. Plus he looked online to see if I have a record. Did you really think he'd let some ax murderer have access to his sister? No way."

She smiled and seemed to relax a little more.

"I know this feels like I'm intruding, but please, don't be angry. Or frightened. I've been through all this before, and I know that you're going to find out it's way harder and way worse than you thought it would be. The doctors never tell you how hard it's really going to be. I know what you're going to be in for, and this is all my fault. I shouldn't have tried to be the hero, but I couldn't see any other way to handle it. Please. I want to help until you're back on your feet." He didn't feel manipulated; all Evan's concerns were justified, which of course only made him feel more guilty.

Her expression softened. "It sounds like you've been through this yourself. What happened?"

He shrugged his shoulders. "Just a few broken bones. But this isn't the time to talk about it. Let's get you settled, and I'll make us both something for lunch."

After he guided her to the couch and helped lift her leg onto the coffee table, complete with a pillow under her heel, Dave made his way to her kitchen.

Her suite was the same layout as his own temporary future home, so as he prepared their lunch he made mental notes of where he would put his own meager kitchen items.

To give her some privacy to process what he'd told her, after he finished making two sandwiches and set them on plates Dave pulled up a chair and watched the coffee machine as the last of the coffee dripped through the filter.

He really needed the coffee since he'd been up most of the night packing and moving. He'd left the main pieces of furniture for his temporary renter, bringing his television and stereo, computer, most of his kitchen goods, and all his personal belongings.

Even though he prided himself on his accomplishment, at the same time it was almost sad that he'd packed and moved virtually everything he owned in one night. He'd even managed to sleep for an hour. He'd been fine all morning, but now that he was no longer trying to beat the clock, the exhaustion was catching up with him.

For one day, he would live out of boxes and unpack after he'd slept. He didn't have a bed, but he did have all his camping gear, including an inflatable mattress, in the trunk of his car. He'd pump it up and sleep on that until he got a real bed.

He must have zoned out, because he noticed the coffee was ready, and he didn't know for how long.

Dave shook his head. He'd just turned thirty—apparently too old to be up all night and still function like a human being the next day.

Ashley didn't know how old he was, but he knew how old she was because her brother had told him. They were both twenty-six, and the birthday of Evan's twins was exactly six months to the day from Ashley and Evan's birthday.

Maybe by her birthday Ashley's life would be relatively back to normal. Until then he would do his best to make things as normal as possible.

He poured two cups of coffee, making hers just as her brother said she liked it, and took their lunches into the living room.

"I would never have thought of putting the couch in the middle of the room like this, but it's a really perfect view both of the television and the window. Maybe I'll keep it like this instead of arranging all the furniture against the walls. Maybe bare walls will become a new trend."

He smiled, maybe for the first time in twenty-four hours. "Then I'm glad to be of service."

She smiled back. "While you were in the kitchen I looked at how you've got all my furniture arranged. I can make it almost all the way to the bathroom using the furniture for balance without crutches."

"My plan is to put a kitchen chair in the empty spot. It looks really odd. That's why I didn't put it there for your first view of what we'd done."

"I guess I really can't be mad at Evan. He's only doing what he thinks will help."

Dave bit his bottom lip. "That's right," he muttered, waiting for her reaction. Truthfully, Evan reminded him of a friend of his mother's.

Ashley closed her eyes and sighed as she bit into the sandwich. "This is so much better than the food in the hospital. I don't know why. It's just a sandwich."

"Maybe it's the atmosphere. And the cook."

She blinked and stared at him like she didn't know what to say, which probably was his cue to leave.

Dave stood. "You're tired. For the next two weeks you're supposed to move your leg as little as possible. So call me, day or night, and I'll be here. Evan already programmed my number into your cell phone. Keep it in your pocket, not your purse, so it's with you at all times. Like I said, except for the obvious, call me any time you need something and I'll be here in under a minute. When it's bedtime, call me and I'll help you get there."

"You really don't have to do this."

"I know I don't have to. I'm doing this because I want to. And Evan's a master guilt-inducer."

She laughed. "Don't I know it."

"All kidding aside, the bottom line is that if it weren't for my actions, you wouldn't need my help or anyone else's. It's my fault you're hurt and I won't feel right until I make it up to you."

He turned and walked to the door. As he opened it he looked at her over his shoulder. "I'll be back at supper time. See you then."

Ashley watched Dave standing in the doorway, looking at her over his shoulder as if waiting for her to say it was okay for him to leave.

She sucked in her bottom lip, nibbled on it, then cleared her throat. "Wait."

One eyebrow quirked. "What do you need?"

She cleared her throat. "I know you've got everything all set up so I can get around by myself, but I'm a little nervous. I don't want to fall down then have to phone you to come and pick me up off the floor. Would you mind waiting while I made it to the bedroom?" She nibbled her lip again, then lowered her voice, looking down at the floor, unable to meet his eyes as she spoke. "Or, I was wondering if you could wait while I went to the bathroom…" The burn in her cheeks told her she was blushing, and he probably could see it. She couldn't believe she'd just asked a man, a near-stranger, to wait for her while she relieved herself, but the washroom at the hospital had bars and supports and lots of space. Most of all, it had a call button for a nurse in case of a mishap.

"No problem."

The door clicked closed, forcing her to look up. "I'm so sorry. I don't want to trouble you, but in case something happens it would be better if you were down here, not all the way upstairs if I have to call you. After I do this once by myself, then I'll feel more confident."

"I don't mind. I took the day off work, so I don't have anything else to do."

Knowing he'd just moved into a new apartment she doubted that were true, but she didn't argue with him.

To her surprise, instead of approaching her to help, Dave leaned against the back of the door, rested one foot over the other, and crossed his arms. "Go ahead. I'll stay here unless you call."

Slowly she rose to her feet, or rather, her one good foot, and using the furniture he'd strewn about, hobbled to the bathroom. As she reached for the door frame to support herself, the couch creaked.

"Take your time," he called out, and the television turned on.

Ashley smiled, then continued on. All a man needed was access to the remote, and time could stand still. Her brother was the same way with the television, as had been Steve.

Ashley paused. She hadn't thought of Steve in a long time, and was sorry that she had now. She didn't know how she could have gone out with him for such a long time and not seen his true colors. He was manipulative and selfish, and always thought of himself first. All the good things he'd done for her weren't really for her; everything had ultimately been to achieve something for his own purposes. If Steve were here today instead of Dave, Steve wouldn't be getting settled on the couch waiting for her just in case she needed something. He'd have been halfway home by now.

As the bathroom light flicked on, her breath caught. A support bar had been fastened to the wall beside the toilet.

Taped to the mirror was a yellow sticky-note with scrawling handwriting.

"Don't worry. I got permission from the landlord."

Her eyes burned, and her throat tightened. A big tear rolled down her cheek, followed by another, then another, until they became a river. If she weren't encumbered, she would have flopped down to sit on the closed toilet seat and had a good cry over Dave's kindness. But all she could do was hop and hobble, unable to swipe her tears away as they ran down her face and onto her blouse. Using the support bar to lower herself onto the closed toilet only made her cry harder.

Once seated, she covered her face with her hands and let herself break down. With any luck, Dave wouldn't hear her over the noise of the television.

She couldn't understand his kindness, which overwhelmed her even more. She hadn't cried after being shot, putting up a brave face in front of everyone, even though for a long time she'd been terrified she wouldn't be able to walk. Probably a psychiatrist could tell her why this was happening now, but she really didn't need to know. She was home, she was safe, and she had time to heal.

Most of all, she had the kindness of a stranger to help her along.

After the tears subsided, Ashley pushed herself up, did what she had to do, washed her face as best she could, and made her way back to the living room.

"Sorry I took so long," she mumbled as she rounded the corner. "I…" Her voice trailed off as she saw Dave collapsed at the end of the couch, his head resting over the back of the couch, his mouth open, his eyes closed.

She couldn't blame him for falling asleep, especially after he'd probably been up most of the night. At least now he wouldn't see her red eyes and ask what was wrong, because she still didn't know.

As best she could, she hobbled to the other end of the

couch and lowered herself gently so as not to rock the couch and wake him.

Once seated, she turned off the television and reached for her book as something quiet to do while he slept. But instead of reading, all she could do was study Dave while he wasn't watching back.

In a worldly sense, he could have been her hero. He could have escaped from the gunman once outside, but instead he'd saved her from being abducted and probably later killed. Yet, during his visits at the hospital, she'd come to know him simply as an ordinary guy, albeit with some very heroic qualities. He'd even gained Evan's trust, which wasn't easy.

He snorted, then began to snore softly.

But realistically, she really wasn't getting to know him. While he'd been cheerful and talkative enough, and their conversations pleasant, they'd never exchanged anything of substance. He was good at coaxing information out of her that fit into general conversation. He already knew more about her than anyone except her pastor and her best friend.

On the other hand, she knew more about his friends who had just gotten married than about Dave Ducharme, the man all the nurses thought was nearly her fiancé. She didn't have a clue as to what made him tick, or why he would have risked his life, then refused to talk to anyone about it. The press had called him The Kung Fu King although he'd later told her it wasn't Kung Fu, it was Tai Kwan Do. He'd refused to speak to the press, or the police. At first the police publicly asked for anyone who knew him to come forward, but they later recanted, saying they had enough witnesses—including herself. Between the staff and other hostages, and the video from the bank, justice would prevail.

As far as she knew his life would go on as normal, whatever his normal was.

Dave shifted slightly, his face tightened, and he stopped snoring, although he didn't awaken. His arms twitched and his face tightened. "No…" he muttered in his sleep, and both legs moved.

Ashley stiffened. She didn't like seeing him have a bad dream. She reached to touch his shoulder to give him a gentle shake when his whole body jolted.

His eyes sprang open, glazed. She touched him as he grabbed her hand, squeezing it hard while his breath came out in quick pants.

"Dave! It was bad dream. It's okay."

His eyes focused. He dropped her hand like it would burn him and pressed himself back in the sofa cushions. "I'm so sorry. Did I hurt you?"

"I'm fine. Are you okay?"

He stood abruptly. "I'm fine. I see you made it back without needing help. I'm sorry I fell asleep. I should go."

She'd barely opened her mouth to say that he didn't have to leave, and he was gone.

Dave stood at Ashley's door, switched the bag of Chinese food to his left hand, and knocked with his right.

The nightmares had started again. That didn't surprise him after being involved in an armed robbery. What did surprise him was that they took so long to start. He'd almost been afraid to go to sleep the first couple of nights after the robbery, but when the dreams he had were good, he thought it was finally over. Obviously it wasn't.

Seeing him as the nightmare was winding up, then fortunately waking him, Ashley hadn't seemed frightened, just concerned. He didn't know if he talked in his sleep; he had no one to tell him if he did or didn't. He didn't want to assume that he didn't. He would never put himself in a position to fall asleep in front of her again.

Instead of using the key Evan had given him, Dave knocked. The key would be used only if she called him, needing help.

"Who's there?" she called from inside.

"It's Dave," he answered back through the door.

"Come in. Do you have your key?"

"Sure do." Because she'd given him permission, he unlocked the door and stepped inside. Once the door closed behind him he held up the bag. "My plans to cook supper didn't work out, so I bought this instead."

She smiled, warming his heart. "I'm glad you were able to sleep. I know you couldn't have slept much last night. Since I know you were upstairs, I hope you didn't go far to pick that up."

He shrugged. "Nope. I didn't go far. There's a place a couple of blocks away called Mrs. Wong's Kitchen. I thought I'd try it out."

"It's pretty good. I get takeout from there often."

He extended one hand toward her. "Don't get up. I'll go get some plates and some milk. We can stay in the living room."

"I like oolong tea with Chinese."

"Oh." He paused. "I was thinking that milk would be better to help your bone heal. I also bought you a big jar of calcium tablets. But you're right, tea is better with Chinese, so I'll make us a pot. But I'd feel better if we had milk later with dessert—if you want."

He waited, expecting her to say *Yes, mother*, but she looked at him instead with an expression like a deer caught in the headlights.

Since he knew where everything was it only took a few minutes, and they were soon eating. They ate in silence for a while, then she set her plate and fork down, and looked at him. "I don't know how to thank you for this. Or for everything else you've done."

He waved his fork in the air, then kept eating. "It's no big deal. Gives me something to do."

"I doubt you have nothing else to do."

"It's true. I don't do much. Go to work and back. Church on Sunday morning. Tai Kwan Do sessions twice a week. Bible study meeting once. That's pretty much it."

As he ate, he tried not to choke on his food, or his words. He'd just summarized his life into four short blips. Was that all he had become?

"Certainly you do more than that."

"Nope."

"I doubt that. What are you doing tonight?"

"Nothing. Just having dinner with you, then I'll go home."

"Then if you have nothing better to do, and since you said you want to help me, I'm already going crazy with cabin fever, I want to go out and do something."

"You're not going to have much fun on crutches. Besides, the doctor said you're not supposed to move around much yet."

Dave looked into Ashley's face. He'd become good at reading people, and from her expression he wondered if she might start to cry. "In the big picture of your life, this isn't long. Only a few months."

"Months?" Instead of the tears he expected, she smacked one fist on the coffee table, then leaned toward him with her palm pressed to the tabletop. "I don't want to feel this way, but I can't help it. It was bad enough being stuck in the hospital, but I accepted that because it was the hospital. I'm home now, and I refuse to be trapped like that in my own living room. I need to go somewhere. Do something."

"It's late, and it's a weeknight. There's really nowhere to go. Especially when you're dependent on crutches. It's really hard on your armpits. You also get really tired, really fast, hauling your weight around like that."

"I need to do something, to breathe in some fresh air."

"You can sit on the balcony."

She shook her head. "I'll feel like I'm stuck in a cage, even worse than the animals at the zoo. Even the zoo animals that need to go outside have grassy fields where they can get out and enjoy the sunshine. I can't do that here unless I sit in the parking lot."

"I don't know what to say."

Her eyes widened, and she broke out into a big smile. "I just got the greatest idea. You said your hours are flexible. They rent wheelchairs at the zoo. Tomorrow, will you take me there? You said you don't get out much. I think it will be a nice break for both of us."

Dave's mind flashed to a mental visual of the zoo. He had never been to the zoo here, but the last time he'd been to a zoo during the daytime on a weekday most of the people there were families with young children, field trips from the schools, and tourists. It was all wide open spaces, and no one paid attention to the other people. Everyone's attention was glued to the animals because that was the reason they were there.

He sucked in a deep breath. "I guess I could. We should go early to avoid the crowds. We can't be too long because I do have work to do." He stood. "I'll clean this up, and I'll go home and check online to see what time they open."

Before she could argue with him, he was on his way.

Chapter 5

Ashley fidgeted in the seat as they waited in the parking lot. "I can't believe there's a line. Why would there be so many people here so early?"

Beside her, Dave shrugged. "It doesn't matter. In a few minutes everyone will be in, and then I'll go get a wheelchair for you."

"I haven't been to the zoo for years, since I was a kid. My family used to come here often. Evan and I used to love visiting the prairie dogs."

"Prairie dogs?" Dave's eyebrows quirked. "But gophers are pests."

She shook one finger in the air at him. "Lots of people make that mistake. Evan and I looked it up. Prairie dogs and gophers are different animals. For one thing, prairie dogs are bigger than gophers. We always thought they were so cute, sitting up and begging for peanuts."

"They weren't begging. That posture is natural for

them. They do that when they sense the possibility of danger."

"In the wild, yes, but in captivity every time we rattled the bag of peanuts, they sat up real fast. But then again, those peanuts might have been quite dangerous. A few of those prairie dogs were really fat."

"That's why they have signs that say not to feed the animals. Including the pests."

"Then why did they sell peanuts? They weren't for the people." Ashley snorted and turned away from Dave to watch the line finally dwindle to a few families and one pre-school group.

Those had been happy days, when she'd come as a child to the zoo with her family. That was before her father's increasing absences. Back then, she couldn't remember their father not being home in the evenings. It hadn't been until she and Evan were in junior high school that that their father began to work late many evenings, and then started to be away the occasional weekend.

They'd believed him when he said it was all about his job, and so had their mother. Only when they started high school and were old enough to understand the nature of relationships, marriage, and deceit, did they begin to doubt him, and by then it was too late. All the damage had been done.

Instead of dwelling on past miseries, Ashley picked up her purse and dug out her camera.

"What are you doing with that?" Dave asked the second she pulled it out.

"I'm going to take a picture of the entrance for Evan. I intend to take lots of pictures today. I even brought an extra battery."

"We're going to make quite a pair, because I brought my camera, too. Take your picture now, while there's no one in front. After you've got a good shot I'll go get the wheelchair."

Ashley waited until there were no people in the frame, clicked, then turned to face Dave. "There, I'm…" Her voice trailed off as she looked at him. During the time she'd taken to compose her photo, Dave had slipped on large dark sunglasses and a baseball cap. If she hadn't been sitting in the same car with him, she wouldn't have known he was the same man she'd come with. She finished her sentence, "…done."

"I'll be right back." Before she could close her mouth, he'd exited the car and was on his way to the main entrance.

She watched as he paid the attendant, then went inside. After a few minutes he came out pushing a wheelchair. Because this seemed like a moment that one day might make a funny story she snapped a quick photo, then slipped her camera back into her purse.

It had been much easier getting into the car than getting out, but with Dave's help she positioned herself in the wheelchair.

"You've got short legs," he said, snickering, as he adjusted the footrests to the right heights.

"I never have to duck for low openings," she muttered back. Not that Dave was so very tall—she'd guess he wasn't quite six feet. Just with her being a little on the short side, at five foot four, he made her feel shorter than usual.

The attendant opened the gate for them at the handicapped entrance, smiling politely as she handed Ashley a map.

"Which way do you want to go?" Dave asked from behind her as he pushed the wheelchair toward a sign pointing to different areas, stepped over to read the sign, then pressed his finger to one of the paths. "Want to do this first?"

"I don't know. Whatever you want. You're driving." Ashley looked up at Dave as he looked down at her. It was an odd perspective. "I feel funny being pushed around. I feel like people are staring, but all they're really doing is giving me a quick look then getting back to their own business. I'm glad you picked this time to come, when it's not really crowded."

"I'm sure that will change in the afternoon, and then it will get really busy in a month when school is out for the summer. For now, let's enjoy the quiet."

The first section he pushed her through was the birds. She enjoyed the happy twittering and took lots of pictures, especially of the colorful parrots. "When we get home we're going to have to compare pictures. I'm finding this is a strange perspective from down here. I'm taking all my pictures from the height of a child."

"I don't know why people think the best shots are from higher up. Often the lower perspective is better. Where you are now, you're getting better shots than me because you're even with that one parrot's face. I'm getting shots of the top of his head."

"I guess." While there were advantages, she would much rather be walking around. Still, she did appreciate the outing more than he'd ever know.

Since they weren't moving, Ashley turned around in the chair and looked up at Dave. This time, up close, with the hat and sunglasses shielding his face, pretty much all she could see was his chin and up his nose.

She really didn't know him well enough to tease him about it. She would never have teased Steve about such a thing—he would have become angry. Despite the fact that she didn't know Dave well yet, she had a feeling he would laugh. Even though he was brave and strong, he also had a kind heart. Otherwise, he wouldn't have brought her to the zoo, of all places. As well, he was very gentle. He was probably the kind of man who would take care of abandoned puppies.

Behind her, she heard the crinkle of the map.

"I want to go into the reptile garden next. This says it's almost time to feed the alligators. You're not squeamish, are you?"

She didn't want to ask what they fed the alligators that warranted such a warning. "I think I'll pass on that. But if you want to see them, go ahead. I'm sure I can wheel myself around." Although she'd heard it was much harder on a person's arms then people usually thought. Maybe she could go find the prairie dogs, and just sit and watch them for a while.

"It's okay. It's healthier to stay outside anyway. Fresh air and all that stuff. How about if I just push you around the large animal path, past the lions and tigers?"

She didn't want to ask if that would be too much work, so she agreed.

All along the path they made pleasant small talk, but every time they got to a new animal exhibit he read the write-up then made a few additional comments about many of the animals. Since he said he didn't get out much, it made her think that he must read a lot.

The next time he read one of the signs, Ashley backed up the wheelchair, then readied her camera to take a picture of him. As she was composing the shot, she studied him in the reflection of the plexiglass cover over the sign.

But when he turned around, he raised his camera to his face, and he took a picture of her as she was taking a picture of him.

He grinned, lowered the camera, then turned back to

the sign. "I've seen more of your camera than I have of you, so I thought I'd do that to preserve my memories of the day."

She sighed. "No, I'm sure you've seen more of the back of my head."

As they continued Ashley got lots of photos of the animals, but she didn't get any more chances to take a photo of Dave, at least not the front of him. Not that she could tell who it was behind the hat and glasses, but she would surely remember this day for a long time.

They were almost at the exit when the movement of a young man to her right caught her eye. She looked at his profile.

Her whole body stiffened, and her heart began to pound. That chin, the straggly blond hair...it was....

The man turned around completely, and she froze, studying his features. The nose was different, and this man's eyebrows were thick.

The wheelchair slowed. "Ashley? Are you okay?" Dave asked from behind her.

She cleared her throat to compose herself. "For a second I thought one of the people in the crowd was the gunman from the bank.

They stopped dead. "Where?"

She pointed at the back of a man watching the monkeys with a little girl, probably his daughter. "Him. But it's not. I don't know why I reacted like that. That guy is behind bars, waiting for trial."

"Yeah. Have you had enough? I think it's time to go."

Ashley would have liked to go to the fishpond, but she wasn't doing any work. Not only had Dave walked around the large grounds, but he'd also had the added work of pushing the weight of the wheelchair, her, and the cast.

Yet, at the same time, even though she'd only been sitting, she felt tired. "Sure, I've seen enough."

Of course they had to exit through the gift shop, even with the wheelchair. As they went through she held back a wave of regret that she couldn't get something to remind her of the day, but then again, she did have dozens of photos.

When Dave had her settled in the car, he pushed the wheelchair back to the gate, where the attendant escorted him in so they could give him back his deposit.

While she waited, Ashley flipped through all the photos on her camera. She had at least one of every animal they visited, and a lot of photos of Dave's back. The only one she had of his front was the one where she was taking a photo of him taking a photo of her.

One day she would find it funny, but today she wished she had a photo of him smiling as they shared the day together.

The car door opened, causing her to flinch.

"Sorry, I didn't mean to startle you."

Ashley pressed her palm over her thumping heart. "I didn't realize I was concentrating so much on my pictures."

He slid in behind the wheel, then held out a bag toward her. "I got this for you. I hope you like it."

Her hands trembled as she accepted the bag, and pulled out a plush prairie dog.

Her voice trembled as she spoke. "Thank you. It's adorable. I love it. You didn't have to."

"I know I didn't. I got it because I wanted to. How about if we get a couple of take-out burgers for lunch?"

"That would be great. It's going to be my treat. Thank you for a simply marvelous day."

"Don't thank me yet. It's only lunchtime. Unfortunately I have some work to do, so after lunch you're on your own. Unless you need me."

She smiled as he backed out of the parking spot, and exited the lot.

"I'll be fine. I've got some email to catch up on, and a pile of books to read. I'm prepared to take it easy, just like the doctor said."

"Super. Now let's go get our lunch."

Dave looked up at the clock, finished one more transaction for his client's account, then began to log off everywhere he'd been.

He hadn't finished what he hoped he'd get done for the afternoon, but his concentration had been compromised.

While he'd seen a similarity between the bank robber and the man who startled Ashley at the zoo, it hadn't been that close. Dave had memorized the gunman's features and would be able to pick the man out of any lineup, or crowd. In his opinion, the man at the zoo hadn't even been close enough to be selected for a lineup.

But Ashley hadn't merely been startled. She'd frozen solid until she made the connection, or rather, the disconnection.

Both the gunman and his partner had been captured by the police, they were in custody, and they weren't connected to any gangs or outside forces. They were merely two desperate punks who thought that robbing a bank was a fast way to get money using their father's gun. Ashley had nothing to be afraid of at the zoo, but fear wasn't rational. She'd still been jumpy in the car.

He'd never know why stuffed animals would be attractive to a grown woman, but the toy helped calm her down, even though it was a rodent.

As he waited for the computer to shut down, Dave

studied the territory of what would be his home for the next few months.

He didn't want to buy new furniture, nor did he want to move everything he had, only to move it back in a couple of months. However one night on an air mattress was enough for him. After he made sure Ashley was comfortable he'd made a quick trip to the store and bought a discount twin-size mattress. With no frame it was on the floor, which perhaps didn't have a lot of class, but it was more comfortable. He'd also bought a cheap desk that he'd assembled in an hour. He still didn't know if he should bother putting some real furniture in the living room, since he wouldn't be spending much time there. Until Ashley was mobile he would be mostly at her apartment when he wasn't working.

For now, he would be making a small detour to her kitchen.

When he'd arrived back at the apartment he'd put a pot roast along with some potatoes and carrots in the oven. He inhaled deeply, enjoying the delicious aroma. Supper was almost ready.

On the plus side, he would be eating much better now that he'd be cooking for two. On the minus side, eating better meant he'd need more exercise.

When the laptop turned off he closed it and tucked it safely away, set the roaster inside a towel lined box, and made his way to Ashley's suite.

Before he knocked he pressed his ear to the door. Only the quiet drone of the television echoed through the door. The drone changed, then changed again.

He smiled. She was bored and was flipping channels.

Dave balanced the box and knocked. "Hey, Ashley. It's Dave. I brought supper. Want me to use the key?"

"Yes, come in."

He didn't even have the door fully closed when she spoke.

"You didn't have to bring supper. I know I'm laid up, but you don't have to do everything for me."

He grinned, held out the box, used the towel to lift the lid of the roaster, then moved the box to let the delicious aromas permeate the air. "I have to eat anyway, and it's much more worthwhile to cook for two than one."

Her mouth opened, then snapped shut.

"Yeah. Doesn't it smell delicious? I know you want it."

Right on cue, her stomach grumbled. She pressed her palms to her stomach, and her cheeks turned charmingly pink. "I don't know how I'm hungry, but I am. If this keeps up, as soon as I'm out of the cast I'll need to be jogging around the block."

"You know that's not going to happen, don't you?"

She sighed. "Yes. It's going to be a long, slow process. I tell myself nearly every hour how much worse it could have been, but it doesn't help."

He turned to the kitchen and started walking. "You stay there. I'll get this cut up and on plates, and we can eat in the living room."

"Since I've been home I've eaten every meal in the living room."

"Then enjoy it. It won't last long. Consider it an adventure."

Before she could reply, Dave made his way into the kitchen and loaded up two plates.

They made pleasant small talk while they ate, mostly about their visit to the zoo, but the whole time, Dave couldn't help but notice Ashley yawning.

Rather than prolong the visit, he quickly gathered the plates and glasses when they were done and made his way back to the kitchen. He found containers to put the food into Ashley's fridge, washed his roaster and was putting it into the box when he heard a whimper from the living room.

He clenched his teeth. He didn't like to think that the scare at the zoo would give her bad dreams, but he knew the drill. Last night was her first night home from the hospital, which also meant the sleeping pills and pain meds were out of her system. Today, for the first time since she'd been shot, her mind was a hundred percent clear.

He left the box in the kitchen and hurried back to the living room to see Ashley seated on the couch, the foot of her casted leg resting on a cushion on the coffee table, her head uncomfortably tilted onto her right shoulder. As she slept her entire body jerked, and her expression was pained.

As gently as possible, he shook her shoulder. "Ashley, you're having a bad dream. Wake up."

She whimpered again. He shook her a little harder. Her head jerked upright, stiffened, her eyes opened wide, and she pressed both palms to her chest. Her breath came out in sharp pants.

"You're at home," he said softly. "It's okay."

Her eyes focused and her body sagged. Her lower lip quivered, then she clenched it between her teeth.

Dave sat down beside her, pulling her close. She didn't protest; instead she leaned into him, so he wrapped his arms around her. He probably should have said some mindless platitudes to calm her down, but he didn't know what to say.

In the background, Sheldon and Leonard argued about some Star Trek minutia while Penny completely missed the point, as usual.

When Ashley straightened and began to move back, Dave released her and stood.

Ashley cleared her throat and sucked in a deep breath. "I can't believe I just had a nightmare about the robbery. I know both of them are in jail. Even if they weren't, they wouldn't come after me. There were plenty of witnesses, plus the video from the bank."

"These kinds of things are seldom rational, although they can sometimes be predictable. I hate to say it, but you'll probably have nightmares for a while, then they'll fade and then it will be nothing but a bad memory. For now, you've got a bit of an adrenaline rush, but once you wind down you'll be tired again and you'll probably want a nap. You'll be more comfortable in your bed. Would you like me to help you get settled? You're probably finding it a little harder to move today than yesterday. I'm going to guess that you haven't had any pain pills today."

"You're right about that. I was going to go to bed, but I thought struggling with the crutches was too much work. I'd really appreciate it if you helped me."

He smiled. "You probably have the crutches set too high. Most people do that. I'll bet the nurses didn't set them for you. Let me fix them for you." He stood and extended one hand to help her get up. Once Ashley was standing he picked up the crutches and handed them to her. "Put the bottoms about six inches to the side from your feet. The best height is when the armrests are about two inches below your armpits." Sure enough, they were three inches too high. After he reset both and returned them to her, he stayed close beside while she made her way to the bedroom.

Once on the bed, Ashley rolled onto her side and struggled to get comfortable. She only had one pillow, and it was under her head. As Dave watched, memories poked at him. "You'll be less uncomfortable with a couple of pillows under your leg." Before she could reply he jogged to the couch and returned with her decorative cushions. He slipped them under her knee and ankle for support, making a mental note to buy a couple of hard pillows next time he was out, which was going to be as soon as he left her place.

While he unfolded a small blanket he'd found in the linen closet Ashley sighed and snuggled her head into the pillow. "You seem to know a lot about bad dreams and broken bones."

Dave stepped back. "I read a lot." Before she asked any questions he didn't want to answer, he laid the blanket over her shoulders and left.

Chapter 6

Ashley stared at the calendar Dave had taped to her living room wall.

Doctor's orders were to move as little as possible for two weeks after the surgery as that period was critical for stabilizing the bone. Keeping still had driven her half crazy, but she'd reminded herself to keep thinking about the big picture.

Tomorrow would be two weeks since the bank robbery. Dave had marked every day on the calendar as time passed as a vivid visual of the day she would be able to move like a semi-normal human being.

In two weeks she'd only been out of her apartment once, and that time was only because she'd agreed to use a wheelchair. Since then, for a major portion of each day Dave had been with her, watching and running every time she needed something. When he was in his own suite, because the clothes she could wear with the cast didn't have a pocket for her cell phone, he'd set up a baby monitor to hear if she had trouble. With him either beside her, or in the next room, or listening from above, he knew when she left the couch and came running to help.

The only time he wasn't on alert in case she needed help was when he went to martial arts classes or to his Bible study meeting. He'd felt too guilty to go to church on both Sunday mornings, so they'd sat together and watched a church service via webcam.

Keeping her butt glued to the couch made Ashley feel like a bear trapped in a cage too small.

She knew every patch of paint on the living room walls and the texture of every thread of her couch.

She'd achieved the highest levels of Bubble Town on her laptop. She'd never been so caught up on email, and she'd organized every file and folder. She'd finished every book in the house, so Dave had loaned her his e-reader. She'd never read so much in such a short time.

One thing that had lifted her spirits was a collection of hand-made cards from her students. Dave had gone to the school to pick up a box from her classroom, and while there he'd taken the time to speak to the children. Many of her students had been traumatized to hear she'd been shot. Most of their parents had seen it on the news and spoken to their families about it before the principal's official announcement, but not all. Dave had taken the time to speak to the class, both as a group and the children individually. He'd assured them all that she was fine and was just waiting for her leg to mend so she could get back to school.

Just.

She'd never been so bored in her life. Evan and Karen had been by a couple of times with the babies, but left as soon as one of them started getting fussy, which wasn't long.

But her home had never been so clean, and her fridge had never been so well stocked.

She also knew that by the time the cast was removed and she could step on the scale, the number would be at least twenty pounds higher from all of Dave's good cooking.

Not only was he a good cook, he also did her house-keeping and laundry, including all the sorting and folding, plus he put everything away sorted by color. Within days, he knew where everything she owned was without looking twice. She'd never known someone so organized, or efficient. After a few days he'd brought his laptop and worked beside her, and he was just as organized and efficient at that, too.

He cooked, he did housework, he was kind and gentle, and he had a good job. One day, Dave would make some lucky woman a good husband. If that woman could somehow dig down and find out what made him tick.

Even though she was getting to know him, she didn't know anything *about* him.

He'd told her that he hadn't grown up in Seattle, but he never said exactly where, only under the broad sweep of the East coast. East Coast? Seattle is on the West;

After learning she was a teacher he had a lot to say about his school where he grew up, but never mentioned the name. Likewise, she knew he'd been to college, obviously he'd taken accounting, but he never said the name of the university.

Yet she knew his birthday, and that he was afraid of spiders and was very embarrassed about it.

She didn't know why he was so evasive. If he didn't want to get personal, that was fine, but living as they had been for the past two weeks, she couldn't have been more personal with him than if she'd been married to him.

Not that she was normally talkative, but spending so much time together being confined to the couch left her nothing to do but talk. She'd found herself talking just so she wouldn't die of boredom.

Despite the strangeness of the situation, or maybe because of it, Dave was easy to talk to. When they weren't talking he'd gone so far as to redo her previous year's income tax, and refiled for a small refund. He knew how much money she made, and where she spent it, to the penny. Her life didn't get much more personal than that.

But she knew nothing about him. Not that she wanted or cared to know his income, but she would have liked to know more than his favorite flavor of ice cream, or that he was allergic to bee stings.

If he wanted to keep his life private that was his business. When he decided that he'd helped her enough they would go their separate ways, and even though he was a very likeable man, she probably wouldn't ever see him again when the current situation was ended.

As a girl, she'd always thought of her father as private as well—quiet and thoughtful, and a bit aloof. Two months before her high school graduation she and her mother had discovered the reason. He wasn't aloof at all. He hadn't been working overtime and traveling for his job for the good of their family. He'd been having an affair—one that had been going on for at least five years.

Instead of moving out when her mother discovered his infidelity, he convinced her to go to counseling even though her mother said she would never trust him again. They were on the way to their second session when they were in a car accident and her mother died. Ashley had later learned that her parents had been arguing in the car, which meant the accident was caused by her father's lack of attention.

A week after the funeral her father moved out and sold the house out from under her and her brother, evicted them from the home they'd grown up in, and disappeared from their lives completely. They guessed he moved to another city with the woman he'd been having the affair with because they couldn't find him. Since she and Evan were no longer minors their father had no legal obligation to support them. Ashley and Evan struggled with the last few weeks of high school and got on with their lives, with a lot of help from the good people at their church.

When the day came that Ashley fell in love and got married there would be no secrets. Her life would be an open book to the man she married. Likewise, that man's life would have to be an open book to her.

"Honey! I'm home!"

She opened her mouth, but no words came out. She wasn't his honey, and this wasn't his home.

He stepped into the living room holding up a bag and a cardboard tray. "I brought coffee and muffins. I'll just get a couple of plates and I'll be right back."

She squirmed to push herself so she directly faced him. "Why are you doing this?"

He blinked. "Because I had to stop at the office this morning. I'm later than usual and I knew you'd be hungry, so I bought the coffee instead of having to wait for it to brew before we could eat."

Ashley shook her head. "That's not what I meant. Why have you been here every day, looking after me? Not that I don't appreciate it. I really do. But why are you doing this?"

His pained expression made her wince. His whole body sagged, and she immediately felt bad at taking the joy out of his moment after he'd done such a thoughtful thing. "I'm sorry," she said. "That really came out wrong. I appreciate everything you've done more than words can say. But I don't understand why you're doing this."

He sighed, set the bag and cardboard tray down on the coffee table, and sat beside her. "Guilt, I guess. It's my fault that you were shot, so it's up to me to help until you're better."

"You've already said all that but it doesn't really explain anything. You make it sound so simple, but it's easier said than done, and it's far from over yet. You've sacrificed so much already."

Dave shrugged his shoulders. "Not really. It's not like I've taken time off work or anything. Like I said, I often work from home this time of year."

"But you've moved out of your home to be closer to me." He couldn't get any closer unless he moved in.

He shrugged his shoulders again. "It's no big deal."

She waited for him to say why it was no big deal, but he didn't.

"You saved my life. If I'd been taken to Mexico as a hostage, he would have killed me. He would never have just let me go."

"I guess that's what I was thinking."

Ashley reached forward and wrapped her hands around one of his. "In comparison to being killed, a broken leg is nothing."

He stared down at their joined hands, making her regret that she couldn't see his face. "It's not nothing. It's terrifying being shot, then once you know you're not dead, you don't know if you're going to be permanently handicapped."

She gave his hands a gentle squeeze. "Yes, it was scary, but when I woke up after surgery the doctor told me that if I looked after myself properly the worst that would happen was a slight limp, and that I probably wouldn't be able to ski again. Which is no big deal, because I've never skied in my life."

"It's still scary."

She lowered her voice. "It hasn't been so scary with you here. Thank you for all you've done."

Still not raising his head, he shifted his hands so they covered hers. "It sounds like you're telling me you don't want me around anymore. If that's what you're saying, I won't come back."

For some reason she didn't understand, her eyes started to burn. She wanted to rub it away, but she couldn't unless she pulled her hands out of his, and she didn't want to do that.

She gulped. "That's not what I'm saying at all. I'd like you to stay."

Dave raised his head and stared into her eyes. "I'd like that, too." He cleared his throat, released her hands, then stood. "I'll go get those plates before the coffee gets too cold."

Before she knew it, he was gone.

Dave pressed his hand to the wall next to the cupboard, squeezed his eyes shut, and sucked in a deep breath. He couldn't believe how his stomach nearly went into spasm when he thought Ashley was telling him she didn't want him around anymore.

He hadn't thought about the possibility that she didn't want him here until she hit him between the eyes.

When he first felt obligated to help as she healed it was completely out of guilt. When someone was hurt, at first lots of people volunteered to help. But people were busy, and as time went on help usually came less and less, even though a person still needed it just as much, if not more, as depression set in.

He wasn't going to desert Ashley when she needed someone. He'd promised to look after her until she was on her feet again. Despite the fact that he'd made that promise to himself and not directly to her it didn't make it any less valid.

But somewhere in the last two weeks, something had changed. He wasn't looking after her out of obligation or even Christian charity.

He was looking after her because he wanted to spend time with her. As he was getting to know her, he couldn't help but like her. She was different from anyone he'd ever known. Of course she was vulnerable right now, both from the injury and the trauma, although no one would know how much trauma until she got back into her real world and routine. A psychiatrist might say he was looking after her like she was an injured bird to work out his own issues, but that wasn't true.

The truth was, he liked her and he wanted to spend time with her. If anything, he was using her injury to his advantage.

It was obvious to him that over the last week she'd been fishing for information about him and his background, and it was probably just as obvious to her that he'd been deliberately evasive.

As a teacher she knew how to coax answers out of a reluctant subject.

Fortunately, he knew the drill.

Before she wondered why he was taking so long, Dave grabbed a couple of plates and returned to the living room.

He cleared his throat, hoping he sounded normal. "I

bought a cranberry muffin for you, and a blueberry one for me. If you want, we can cut both in half and share."

She smiled, doing strange things to his already confused digestive system. "I'd love to split them."

Cutting them both in half gave him an excuse to speak to her without having to look at her. "Since tomorrow is officially two weeks, that means it's time for you to get mobile. What would you like to do?"

She rested her fingers on the back of his hand, forcing him to stop cutting, and look up. "I was planning to go to the mall when everything went wrong, so that's what I'd like to do. Go shopping."

The look on her face was like a kid in a candy store. However, what she was asking wasn't realistic.

"That's not a very good idea. You've already found out the hard way that getting around on crutches isn't as easy as people think. Can't you pick something else?"

She shook her head. "I've already thought that same thing. But before I go anyplace I need to buy some new clothes. For starters, some longer skirts that are more roomy. Also, I need some shorts that are stretchy, so I can pull them up over the cast." She shuddered. "I don't know when it dawned on me that I'm going to have this cast all summer long. I've got nothing to wear."

"There's nothing wrong with what you've been wearing."

"All I've been wearing is my old sweatpants. They're fine for around home, but not to go out in public."

He opened his mouth to protest, to tell her that with a cast, fashion wasn't an issue. No one would care about her paint-stained sweatpants. But before the words came out, he could see disappointment starting to come over her.

Dave let out a sigh. "Okay. Tomorrow I'll take you to the mall."

She smiled, causing his brain to short-circuit. "Great! Can you reach my laptop? I want to show you ~~want~~ what I want to buy. Let's eat first, and then we can do some surfing."

Chapter 7

"Are you sure you're ready for this?"

"Yes, of course," she said, but now that they were in the mall parking lot, she wasn't quite so sure.

The only other time she'd been outside of her apartment since the robbery had been when Dave had taken her to the zoo. She'd struggled getting to the car despite going very slowly, but she hadn't needed to consider going any farther. At the zoo Dave had brought the wheelchair right to the car, and after that he'd been the only one expending any effort.

Today, she didn't want a wheelchair. As well, today she'd have an audience—an audience of strangers, but an audience none the less.

Instead of pulling into a handicapped parking spot, Dave stopped the car in front of one of the store entrances. "I'm going to let you out here because I won't park in a handicapped spot without an authorized hangtag. This is where you wanted to go, right?" He pointed to the door that led into one of the department stores, versus the mall entrance.

"Yes." Besides being her favorite store, the section for ladies' clothing was right by this door.

Ashley couldn't help but turn and look at one of the designated handicapped parking spots where there was already a car parked. No blue permit card hung from the rearview mirror. As she stared, a woman without a limp, her arms loaded with shopping bags, sauntered to the car, opened the trunk, tossed everything in, then got in the car and drove off.

She'd seen it before and been annoyed, but suddenly now she felt angry. While she didn't have a temporary handicap hangtag and couldn't use the space, she now had more empathy for people who really were disabled. On television when the hero of the show was injured and on crutches they made it look so easy. It wasn't easy at all.

Ashley vowed to herself that in the future she would start writing reminder notes and leave them under the windshield wipers when people who weren't handicapped parked in the handicapped spots. She probably could get the youth group from her church to join her in a crusade to keep the spots reserved for those who really needed them. However, she didn't want to cause an altercation. No one could know what kind of nutcase had a gun. She didn't ever want to see anyone with a gun outside of a shooting range.

Maybe she'd report cars like that to the store, so they could call a tow truck.

"Ashley? Are you okay? Do you want to go home?"

Ashley felt her cheeks heat up. "Sorry. I was lost in thought. What did you say?"

"I said I can let you out here so you can sit on the bench to wait for me. I'll be back as soon as I find a parking spot. But you might be waiting for a while. The lot is packed."

Ashley turned her head to survey the lot. Except for the recently vacated handicapped spot, she couldn't see an open spot anywhere. If the outside of the mall was mayhem, she could imagine the inside of the mall was the same. "Maybe Saturday wasn't the best day to come here."

He turned to face her. "Do you want to go home?"

She noticed that he'd asked the same question twice, which told her that he was the one who wanted to go home. However, she feared if she didn't do this today she would lose her nerve. "No. I need to go shopping and I have to get away from my apartment." She would go crazy if she had to wear her paint-stained sweatpants another day or stare at her walls without at least a short break. "Let's go in."

Just like at the zoo, Dave helped her out not very gracefully, nearly hauling her out of the car by her armpits. Then, instead of handing her the crutches like she expected, Dave slipped one arm around her waist, held both crutches with the other, helped her hobble to the wooden bench, and lowered her to the seat.

"I'll be back as soon as I find a parking spot."

She couldn't help but smile. "It's not like I could go very far, even if I wanted to. You know where to find me."

He didn't smile back. He just nodded, returned to his car, and drove off.

While he was gone Ashley did something she'd never done before—probably because she'd never sat for very long while in or near a mall. She watched the crowd around her.

It seemed to be a typical Saturday crowd. Most of the shoppers were groups of teen girls and boys glued to their cell phones and not talking to each other as they walked. Many young couples and a few older ones, some walking hand in hand, entered the mall actually speaking to each other. A few young mothers pushed babies in strollers with other children trailing along.

Of the people who were alone, there were more men than women.

Ashley's attention was drawn to the unaccompanied men as they walked through the mall doors. Of all the men she knew, none liked to shop. Most had their wives or girlfriends do their shopping for them just so they could avoid the mall. Maybe instead of shopping these lone men had other plans, perhaps to meet someone in a convenient place. Not that the mall, with today's lack of parking, would be a good choice for that.

Or maybe, instead of fighting the crowd, they wanted to take advantage of it. It would be easy for a lone person to get lost in the crowd today. Just like no one had thought anything unusual of the man who had entered the bank on a busy Saturday with a robbery in his plans, no one would know if someone came in today to rob the jewelry store. A robber wouldn't need to run far to escape. He or she could simply slow to the same pace as everyone around them and get lost in the crowd without having to try very hard. Although on a hot day like today no one was wearing a jacket that could conceal a weapon.

But the thought of a concealed weapon made her watch the lone men a little closer. Many men wore loose shirts, which could conceal a small handgun. And, it didn't have to be a man. A woman could carry a concealed weapon as well. Not every woman wore skin-tight clothing and most of them had handbags.

All that was needed was the threat of one bullet, or not just a threat, one shot, not even aimed at a person, to do a lot of harm. In today's crowd it would cause a stampede. Instead of just one person being shot, many victims would also be trampled.

Ashley shuddered and tried to think of something else. That day at the bank was a rare, one-time occurrence. Or, at least she hoped it was. She simply had been in the wrong place at the wrong time. The chances of being in another armed robbery were slim to nonexistent.

"Sorry I took so long. I couldn't find a close parking spot."

Ashley flinched at Dave's voice, turned her head to look up at him, then froze.

If she hadn't recognized his voice, she wouldn't have known it was him.

"How many baseball caps do you own?"

He grinned. "Lots."

"Sunglasses, too?" She could barely see his face behind the large glasses.

He shook his head, no longer grinning. "Nope. Just two. I always wear the same pair, but I have a spare set in the glove compartment."

She tried to shake the feeling that he could have been in the numbers of men she'd just deemed suspicious. She told herself she was just being paranoid. Nothing was going to happen today.

Besides, she had no intention of being in the middle of the crowd. Especially now that her eyes had been opened to the risks.

Dave helped her to her feet, then waited while she maneuvered the crutches to the right position. When she got herself properly balanced they slowly made their way to the door.

For only a second Dave stepped ahead to press the handicap button for the automatic door. While it engaged he pulled open the other door to make the gap wide enough so they could pass through together, side by side.

"Be careful, those shiny tiles can be slippery."

Part of her told herself to slow down. Another part said she was already going so slow she couldn't go any slower unless she stopped. A third part of her wondered what had happened to him that he should warn her.

As soon as the doors closed behind them, Dave plucked off his sunglasses and slid them into his pocket. The baseball cap stayed on, and if she weren't mistaken, he pulled the brim down a little bit.

She wished she could point, but she couldn't. Instead, she motioned with her head. "We're going over there. You're okay going into the ladies' wear department, aren't you?"

"Don't worry. I'm not shy. Although, there are a few ladies' departments I won't go into. So if you want that, then I'm outta here."

Even if she did wander into the wrong department, she had a feeling he would remain beside her. But she didn't want to embarrass him. Not only that, she was already starting to feel tired, and they hadn't even arrived at the right aisle.

"What do you want to buy?"

"Sweatpants. Without holes or paint stains." In one more week Natasha would be back and she could go on a real shopping trip. Natasha would go into the changing rooms with her and help actually try things on. For today she would hold up the pants in front of her, make sure they were large enough, and it was a sale. Except she didn't know how she could do that when she had to use her hands to support herself on the crutches. "That's all I want."

His eyes lit up. "Really? You don't want to go shopping for shoes or anything?"

"Do I look like I need shoes? Although I need a few pairs of warm socks." She wiggled the toes of her right foot. "Even though my leg feels warm, my toes are cold."

"That's normal. Thick socks will solve that. It's a good thing this isn't the middle of winter. That would be even worse."

He helped her to the section where the sweatpants were stacked in piles on a shelf, and in a very gentlemanly manner didn't ask what size she wore. When he saw her struggling with balance as she tried to hold a pair up to herself he hesitated, then removed the pants from her hands.

"Is this what you want to do?" he asked as he grasped the pants by the hips and without pulling or stretching the fabric, held them up to her.

"Those would fit okay, but do you think the leg will fit over the cast?"

"I'm not sure. It would work better if you picked a larger size that has a drawstring in the waist. They'd be baggy, but they would be easier to pull on over the cast."

"This isn't formal wear or a fashion statement. As long as it covers me, I'm good." She needed to buy a few longer, loose flowing skirts, but that was for another day.

He selected a larger pair of sweatpants, held them up, then nodded. "This is good. What else do you want to get?"

Ashley motioned her head to the next aisle. "Fuzzy socks. Then we can go home."

He draped the pants over his arm, waited for her to go in the right direction, then stayed beside her, ready to catch her if she lost her balance negotiating between the aisles until she reached an end display of fuzzy socks.

While he waited for her to pick the right ones, if it wasn't her imagination, it seemed like the ball cap rode higher on his head, and she could actually see all of his face.

As if he could tell she was thinking about him and the hat, he grasped the bill with his thumb and forefinger, and tugged it back down.

She couldn't stop herself. She turned her head and stared into his eyes. "Why do you wear that thing all the time when we're not at home? It's not like you've got a bald spot you're trying to hide."

He shrugged his shoulders. "I don't know. Habit, I guess. Besides, it's comfortable."

As far as Ashley was concerned, however comfortable any hat could be, once removed it didn't leave a person's hair in good order. The expression "hat head" was exactly for situations like this. The fashion statement of the hat wasn't worth the resulting hat head.

Yet Dave was never untidy, and she'd never seen that his hair needed washing when he took off the cap. His hair and clothes were clean and well kept. He wore jeans in good condition, and on the days he stopped at his office first he showed up wearing pressed dress pants and a neutral shirt that were well matched.

If she were selecting his clothes she would choose something with more color for him. Dave was certainly a good-looking man and needed to dress with more pizzazz. The first time she'd seen him at the bank wearing the tuxedo, hers wasn't the only female eye he'd caught. At the time she'd thought it amusing that he'd seemed awkward knowing ladies of all ages were watching him before the robbery diverted everyone's attention to the crisis. Now that she'd gotten to know him a little she'd learned that he was always like that. He avoided crowds and kept to himself, but at the same time, wearing the hat and sunglasses every time he went out in public seemed extreme.

She had no idea why a handsome man like Dave wouldn't want people looking at his face. While she was thinking about it, when he wasn't looking she checked more closely for scars, and there were none. Although often the worst scars were deep inside, where no one could see.

Deep down, Dave had scars.

She didn't want to think that he avoided contact with people because he'd been a victim of child abuse, but as an elementary school teacher she was trained to look for warning signs.

Whatever painful secrets he held, she wanted to coax him to open up to her, and by doing so, begin the path to healing and restoration. Not here, but when they got home, she would do that.

He'd put a large portion of his life aside to help her, and she was going to do the same for him.

No matter how long it took, she would help.

Dave added a bit more milk to the potato mixture, mashed it again, then set the pot aside. As he stirred the gravy, he ran his fingers over the notches of his belt. Years ago he'd been a good cook, and his waistline had shown every ounce. He hadn't cooked like this for a long time. Cooking with all the extras lost its appeal when only doing it for one. Now that he was cooking for two he found he hadn't forgotten a thing. Unfortunately, he also hadn't forgotten how difficult it had been to get his weight down, and even harder, to keep it down.

Tonight, after Ashley was settled he needed to go to his real home—or at least to the building's basement to spend some time in the fitness room. Then, on Monday, he'd go back to his normal routine of biweekly sessions at the martial arts studio for a full workout.

He couldn't afford to get sloppy. He'd already gained a pound, and it had only been two weeks.

He picked up the fork to flip the pork chops in the frying pan, then wondered why he was cooking pork chops with gravy when he should have chosen chicken cutlets with lemon sauce. Until he had to watch his own weight he'd scoffed at the way so many women counted every calorie and stressed over a morsel of chocolate. Now he was no different. Of all the things in his life that had changed, unfortunately his metabolism wasn't one of them. He needed to exercise. And he could only do that alone.

He didn't know if Ashley was so thin because she also kept up a personal exercise regimen, or if unlike him, she had been blessed with a fast metabolism. Either way, not only for himself, but also for her sake, he needed to make careful meal choices. Even though Ashley was no longer strictly confined to the couch, her level of activity wasn't going to improve for another six weeks. Or, depending on how the break healed, or didn't heal, it could be as long as six months. Only time and more X-rays would tell.

For now, casted from ankle to mid-thigh, she wouldn't be going too far too fast. His best exercise would be rushing ahead to open doors. Her natural build was slim and tiny. If she put on weight then managing the crutches would be even more difficult for her.

Today they could have the pork chops with mashed potatoes and gravy, accompanied by broccoli with melted cheese sauce.

Tomorrow he would make chicken with salad.

He was almost ready to put everything on plates when the telltale thumping of the crutches approached.

He turned as Ashley entered the kitchen. When the tip of the crutch made contact with the floor it slipped a few inches, making her momentarily lose her balance. Her eyes widened and she leaned her shoulder to the side to bump into the wall rather than fall. Once stable, she righted the crutches under her arms, continued on her journey to the table, then dropped into one of the chairs.

She sighed as she rested the crutches against the edge of the table. "I keep forgetting about the difference between the texture of the carpet and the slippery floor."

"Just wait until you're out at a friend's place and they have a throw mat somewhere. When you're walking normally you never think about it, but when you're on crutches they fly right out from under you. What happens next isn't a pretty picture. No one ever thinks to move those things, even though they know you're coming. And you never think about them until it's too late, because they've always been there. I know this the hard way."

She winced. "Did you hurt yourself?"

"No new breaks, but I sure felt like an idiot." Worse, for a few days his arm hurt so much he could barely use the crutches. But he'd already felt like a caged animal, so he'd gritted his teeth and carried on.

"Something smells really good. I think I'm getting spoiled."

From the stock she'd had in her kitchen before he went shopping, he could see that when living alone, she normally ate like he did. "Don't get used to it. It won't last. Neither of us can afford to get fat, so starting tomorrow we're both going to be eating light."

She blinked suddenly at his word *fat*. Rather than explain, he turned his head, pulled two plates from the cupboard, and started putting out the food.

"Do you have any plans for tonight? I don't want to keep you from doing what you normally do."

"No plans," he replied without hesitation.

"Really? It's been two weeks, and you've been here every evening with me instead of your friends or family. You said you did martial arts twice a week, but you've only gone once. You also missed your last Bible study meeting."

"I'm going back to martial arts next week, Mondays and Thursdays. Bible studies have pretty much wrapped up for the summer. It's June, after all. Ball season."

"You're absolutely sure?"

"I'm sure. No plans." Not tonight, not for most nights.

"Then would you mind if Tasha came over? I just got an email from her and she's finally settled in from her trip. She wants to come over and see me, and she's absolutely dying to meet you."

For a second, Dave froze. It made sense, even though he didn't want to be interviewed by a well-meaning friend. However, his friend Tyler had tried for a while to be a matchmaker. However, he had soon set Tyler straight. "I guess that's okay."

"Do you have a friend you'd like to call? After all, it'll be the two of us girls, and you."

"I can't call anyone on short notice like this." He turned to her, grinned, and quirked one eyebrow. "Besides, it sounds like fun, spending the evening with two lovely ladies. Every single man's dream."

Ashley snorted. "Good luck with that. It's not like we'd go out for a night of dinner and dancing where you'd have a woman on each arm. But Tasha would be open for that, just the two of you."

Dave opened his mouth, but he stopped before saying anything out loud.

He'd almost made a glib comment about wanting exactly that. He couldn't remember the last time he'd been out in an open public party atmosphere. But thinking about it, what flashed in his mind wasn't being with the potentially gorgeous Tasha. He'd pictured himself in a crowd, having fun, with his arm around Ashley, smiling down at her as she smiled up at him.

He lowered his head and finished spooning the cheese sauce on top of the broccoli. "We're already having dinner at home," he muttered.

"I didn't mean that having dinner with you wasn't going to be fun. I just didn't want to tie you down. If there's someone else you'd rather spend your time with on Saturday night…"

Dave forced himself to smile, then set the two filled plates on the table. "I already told you, I'm single. There's no one else I'd rather spend a Saturday night with than you."

As he lowered himself into the chair, he told himself not to think about how true those words had become.

It wasn't just that he'd been single too long, or that his best friend had just gotten married to a really nice woman, reminding him what he was missing.

Even though he'd only known Ashley for two weeks he was already becoming very fond of her. He hadn't missed his usual routine at all. In fact, she'd even dragged him out of that routine. He couldn't believe he'd given in so easily and gone to the mall on a busy Saturday. Of course they'd only gone in one store and had left within half an hour. Technically, though, he hadn't known that the trip would play that way until it was over and they were on the way home.

"Can I ask you something?" Ashley plunked her elbows on the table, leaned forward, and rested her chin in her palms. "If it's too personal, just tell me to mind my own business."

"Sure." Dave gritted his teeth and prayed she would ask a question he could answer.

"You know a lot about having a broken leg, but you've never told me what happened."

He clenched his lower lip in his teeth. He'd rehearsed his story enough times that it should have come out easily, except Ashley deserved better than that. Only he didn't know how much to say.

"I fell off a bridge. Jumped, actually."

She stared at him, probably expecting him to say more, except he'd said too much already. "What happened? Weren't there any guard rails or anything? Or was it an accident?"

"No accident. I did it on purpose. It wasn't a really high bridge, but high enough. The jump was easy. It was the landing that was hard."

"Why did you jump off a bridge? I don't see you as being the daredevil type."

"I'm not usually. It just seemed like a good thing to do at the time. Now let's eat before this gets cold. Would you like to say grace?"

Chapter 8

Ashley sat at the table while Dave washed the dishes.

Tonight she'd started with one question, except instead of finding any answers, it only opened more questions.

She couldn't imagine Dave jumping off a bridge. Yet at the same time, she couldn't see him confronting an armed bank robber, yet he'd done exactly that.

He didn't say he was pushed. He had jumped.

She had no idea why anyone would choose to do that.

She didn't want to buy into stereotypes, but accountants didn't traditionally take risks.

It didn't make any sense. A man who was afraid of spiders jumped off a bridge. Maybe there was a spider on the bridge? Ashley shook her head to rid herself of that ridiculous thought.

He'd chosen a career with little need to contact other people, a day-to-day life that by nature was quiet. If he was a victim of something that made him have difficulty dealing with people the life of an accountant would suit him.

But he had no difficulty that she'd seen. At the bank when he walked in wearing a full tuxedo all female heads had turned. He met everyone who looked at him with a smile, sometimes bordering on flirtatious. He'd faced down the bank robber with no difficulty, even tried to reason with the man to stop the robbery.

Whatever Dave was, he wasn't shy, nor was he afraid of people.

Just as Dave finished drying the pan the buzzer for the front door sounded.

"That would be Tasha. Can you let her in? The black button opens the front door."

Dave picked up the phone, greeted her friend, laughed, then pushed the button.

No, the man was not shy.

Ashley pushed herself up, got the crutches in the right place and aimed herself toward the door.

Of course Natasha knocked before she was halfway there.

Dave jogged around her and let her friend in.

He extended one hand. "I'm Dave. I'm obviously not a recording."

Tasha looked down at his hand, then up at his face. "Wow," she muttered, smiled, then slowly reached forward to return his handshake. "You look just like the picture."

He froze. "What picture?"

When Natasha started digging through her purse Ashley wished there were somewhere she could run and hide. If she could run.

Natasha pulled out her phone, pushed a few buttons, then held it up to Dave. "See? Ashley did a sketch and took a picture of it and sent it to me. I think it's a really good likeness. She should work for the police department doing sketches for witnesses."

Dave frowned. "That's all done digitally now."

Ashley cleared her throat. "Dave, this is Natasha, otherwise known as Tasha. Now that you've been formally introduced, let's go sit down so we can talk."

Dave nodded. "Sure. Would anyone like some tea?"

Without waiting for an answer, he turned and disappeared into the kitchen.

As Dave went into the kitchen, Natasha's mouth gaped open. "He's making you tea?"

"No." Ashley raised one finger to her lips to silently tell her to speak softly. "He's being a good host and making *us* tea."

Natasha lowered her voice to a stage whisper. "That's not what I meant. You said he's been making you supper every day. I see he's cleaned your place, too, because it sure doesn't look like this normally. He brings you tea. Does he also do your laundry?"

Ashley nodded. "It's so embarrassing. He says he's got a sister so he's seen everything before, but that doesn't really help." She was about to tell her friend that he'd organized all her cupboards so she could reach the things she needed, but before she could continue Natasha grabbed one arm and started shaking it.

"He does your laundry? Are you serious? Why haven't you married him?"

Ashley freed her arm and waved one hand between them. "It's not that simple. I don't really know him very well yet." Although admittedly she knew him better after two weeks than some people she'd known for years. "It's not wise to marry someone after only two weeks."

Natasha leaned toward her. "I have an idea. Work on it. He sounds like a keeper."

Strangely, the nurse at the hospital had said the same thing. Yet he was still single. Or at least he claimed to be. "There's something I can't put my finger on with him. He's great to talk to and he's doing so much to help me, but out in public it's like he's a different person. He suddenly becomes almost silent and it's like he's always watching over his shoulder. But that's not exactly it, either. At the zoo he talked to children about the animals, and even read the information boards to some of them. But he didn't talk to any of the other adults. In fact, he always wears a hat and sunglasses when he's outside. He says he's sensitive to getting sunburn, but I think there's more to it than that. It's like he doesn't want anyone to see his face."

Natasha's eyes widened. "Maybe he's a secret agent! On a top secret mission!"

"Shh!" She waved her hands in front of her again, trying once more to signal Natasha to keep her voice down. "He's not a secret agent. He brings his work here to do sometimes. He's an accountant. I've talked to his boss."

"You did what?"

She pressed one finger over her lips. "Before I was released from the hospital Dave said he wanted me to trust him, so he brought a letter of reference from his boss, on company letterhead. When I got home I looked them up in the phone book to make sure it was real, then I called to make sure it was legit. It is. His boss is actually quite nice. He also said he's fine with Dave doing his work off-site, which apparently means at my place. And you know Evan. He also checked him out thoroughly."

"About that, you said he moved in upstairs to be closer to you. I hate to say this, but you know what your dad did. He had two addresses, and two families. Even though the other woman knew about your mom and the kids, your mom didn't know about them. Could he be doing the same thing?"

All the things her father managed to hide for so many years flowed through Ashley's mind like a waterfall. Everyone had believed him when he said he was working late and doing out-of-town sales calls. They all thought he was doing so much for the family he allegedly adored. He had a good excuse for everything, but when one small crack broke in his carefully constructed wall the lies and deceit cascaded through like a tsunami, drowning them all. "No. Evan went to Dave's place when I was in the hospital. His real place. Evan says it's quite nice and very obviously the home of a single man who lives alone and spends a lot of time there. He said he sublet it to an exchange student while he's living upstairs."

"You said he's got a sister. Have you met her or anyone in his family yet?"

"That's the thing. He says he's got a sister, but that's all I know. I don't know her name, where she lives, or even where Dave is from. I don't know where he grew up or which university he went to. He never talks about that kind of stuff. I don't know if his parents are still alive or where they live. Nothing. It's weird."

Natasha grinned. "It's only been two weeks. Give it time."

"That may be true, but it's been a long two weeks. He's here most of the day, every day."

Natasha leaned back, crossing her arms over her chest. "Really?"

"He said he wanted to take care of me while I'm trapped sitting on the couch, and that's exactly what he's doing. Only it's not business like a nurse. It's become very personal. When he's not doing his job on the kitchen table he's here in the living room with me. We've been spending a lot of time together. He's so interesting to talk to and we enjoy so many of the same things."

One eyebrow quirked. "Oh?"

"Earlier this week there was a *MythBusters* marathon on TV. You know how much I love that show. It's his favorite show, too. We had this huge debate about the episode where they tested the myth that a duck's quack doesn't echo. It does echo, except the echo gets lost in the quack, and that's why people can't hear it. Even the computer barely detected it. We put it on Pause and spent over half an hour debating parameters of when it no longer matters. It can't be a real echo if even a specialized computer can barely detect it."

"And you're telling me this because?"

This time Ashley lowered her voice. She checked over her shoulder to make sure Dave wasn't coming back yet, then leaned closer to her friend. "We're never at a lack for conversation. He's an expert on interesting trivia, and his delivery just keeps me hooked. He's really in the wrong profession. He should have been a teacher. He's got such a gift for keeping even minute details interesting. He just makes me want to know more. I don't even notice that he hasn't answered any of the questions I asked him until he's gone and it's too late." She almost had said that it didn't matter anymore, but it had happened so often, it was starting to matter. She was getting to know him, but she didn't really know anything *about* him.

Natasha's face hardened. "For most guys, talking about themselves is their favorite topic. Unless they have something to hide."

"I know," Ashley muttered. "It's almost like he's doing it on purpose. Either that or we're both too easily distracted."

"I guess the best I can say is to be careful. Maybe he's a

rich foreign prince who needs to prove to his parents that he doesn't need their immense wealth to live a good life."

"He's not a foreign prince. He's got no accent or anything. He's even an organ donor."

"After knowing a guy for two weeks, you've discussed what to do if either of you are in a fatal accident?"

Ashley shook her head. "No, nothing like that. It says on his driver's license that he's an organ donor. He gave me a copy when he gave me the letter of reference from his boss. He said if he were in my position he'd have a hard time trusting me, so he did all that so I would feel safe. I know everything about him that counts—his address, his place of employment, even his height, weight, and date of birth."

"Have you just outright asked him where he's from? What about—"

"Shh. Here he comes." Ashley smiled at Dave as he rounded the couch holding two cups of hot tea.

He set one cup in front of each of them, then turned to Natasha. "I don't know how you usually like your tea, but this is a good herbal blend that I'd encourage you to try first without adding any sugar or milk."

Ashley forced a smile. "Did I tell you that Dave put me on a diet today?"

Natasha's mouth dropped open. "A diet? You don't need to diet." She turned to Dave. "What are you? Some kind of control freak?"

Dave shook his head. "It's not a diet. I just said we needed to be really careful with what we eat for a while. It's too easy to put on weight when movement is restricted. It's hard enough for Ashley to get around as it is. A few extra pounds would make that even harder, and it's going to be a long time before that cast comes off. When it does, she'll still be on restrictions for a long time."

A silence hung around them while Natasha considered his words. "That makes sense. I guess." She rubbed her hands together. "So tell me a little bit about yourself, since you're a bit of a local hero now, and you're spending so much time with my best friend. I already know you're an accountant. Where are you from? Where did you go to school?"

Ashley waited for Natasha to ask if he was married. Thankfully she didn't.

Dave frowned and looked down at the coffee table instead of up at Natasha when he answered her. "I wouldn't call myself a hero. I just helped get the thief arrested sooner, that's all. With all the bad stuff that's been happening with firearms in this country, this was barely a blip in the radar. No explosions, not a lot of people involved, it was just an attempted robbery, and nothing was even stolen. In the big picture, it certainly didn't rate hero status."

"I think it did. There were nearly two dozen people held hostage."

For this, he finally looked up. "Actually it wasn't that many. It was seventeen plus me and Ashley."

"That's still a lot. It didn't say in the newspaper exactly how many people were involved, or on the news that night."

He shrugged. "I counted. Numbers are my business. Accuracy is important. Did Ashley tell you that I redid her income tax and found enough to get her a $287.48 refund?"

Natasha turned to Ashley. "You didn't tell me that."

Dave smiled. "If you want, I can look over yours. Did you do it yourself, or have a professional do it for you?"

Natasha's cheeks darkened. "My mother does it for me."

"Unless your mother is a tax specialist, then that's all

the more reason for me to at least go over last year. Would you like to make an appointment? Or if you want it might be a nice outing for Ashley for the two of us to go to your place one evening. Unless the only access you have is stairs."

"It's only up three stairs to get up to the front door. After that, the kitchen and living room are one level. You can do that, can't you Ash?"

Ashley nodded. She didn't even have to speak. As soon as Natasha saw the positive answer, she turned back to Dave and started talking to him as if Ashley wasn't even there.

As Dave and Natasha talked about the ins and outs of Natasha's tax issues, Ashley couldn't stop herself from grinning. By the time they finished dissecting Natasha's financial history to see if she could get more deductions Natasha would never remember to get back to her original questions.

Dave had done the same with herself, more than once. All conversations had turned quickly and naturally away from Dave. It was all so natural she didn't feel he was being evasive on purpose, except that by now it had happened so often it raised her suspicions.

When they were done talking taxes she joined the conversation until it turned again to *MythBusters,* and Natasha began to yawn.

"That herb tea is good," she mumbled at the close of her yawn, "but it's not doing anything to keep me awake after a busy week. Besides, I need to get up early in the morning for church."

"Not that early," Ashley countered.

"Early enough. Are you coming?"

In her mind, Ashley pictured the entrance, including a lot of stairs. "I'm not sure. The building has a handicapped entrance somewhere, doesn't it? I don't even know, I've never thought about it before."

From the look on Natasha's face, she didn't know either.

"If you want," Dave said, "I can take you to my church. Unlike your church, it's quite small. We don't video the services like your church so it's not recorded or live on webcam for anyone to see anywhere in the world, and our worship team only has four people. If you're okay with low-tech, it's a nice group of people, probably about a hundred-and-fifty or so in the congregation if everyone is there. The pastor is a homey kind of guy, more like a friend than a teacher when he presents a sermon, if you're in for that kind of preaching. But most of all, it's a level entrance."

Ashley paused. Most of the people at church knew each other at least by face, although most of them only saw each other on Sunday mornings. A number of them had helped her and Evan after their mother died and their father deserted them. But for the most part, aside from her Bible study group she didn't know that many people that well. If only half of the thousand people who attended every Sunday morning came to wish her well, that was still five hundred people, which was about four-hundred-ninety-nine more than she wanted to talk to about being held hostage at gunpoint and then shot.

She didn't think she was ready for that.

"A level entrance sounds good."

He turned to Natasha. "Would you like me to walk you to your car?"

"Naw, I'm parked right in front. You can watch me through the window if you want."

"I want."

As he'd said, as soon as the door closed he walked to

the window, waited while Natasha took the elevator to the ground floor, then watched through the blinds until the horn honked, meaning Natasha was driving away.

"I think it's time for me to get going, too. The service starts at ten, so I think we should leave at nine-thirty. Is that okay with you?"

"Since your church is small, everyone probably knows each other pretty well. Does everyone know what you did at the bank?"

"No. The only ones who know are the pastor and my friends Tyler and Brittany, and I intend to keep it that way. No one will know who you are except for my friends. I'm sure a lot of people will express sympathy for the broken leg, but no one will gush over you about the robbery. The only photo of you from that day was you being loaded into the ambulance, and that didn't show your face. No one will recognize you."

She couldn't believe how good it felt to hear that. "Then I'll see you at nine-thirty. Don't be late."

Chapter 9

"God bless you all, and go in peace."

Dave opened his eyes after the pastor's prayer, and sighed.

For another Sunday the service was over and it was time to get back to his real life. Not for the first time, he was in no rush to go. Here, he knew everyone, maybe only on the surface, but there were no strangers. Any newcomers were usually families, or for those other singles walking in for the first time, they were relaxed and obviously there to step back from the Monday-to-Friday rush. For the most part, with the low-tech or no-tech service, this was a crowd of easygoing people. Anyone wanting more usually only came once. At the end of a service that still used an obsolete overhead projector instead of computer-generated PowerPoint displays, they never stopped to talk to anyone, but just left knowing this wasn't what they wanted in a church.

It was exactly what Dave needed. No strangers, no surprises.

But he had a surprise for everyone else. For the first time since he'd been a member here, which was coming up five years, he hadn't come alone. Not only was he not alone, he was with a woman.

Everyone would want to check Ashley out, and many probably had been itching in their seats for the duration of the entire service, waiting to meet her.

In order not to overwhelm Ashley, Dave remained in his chair until most of the congregation had filed out into the foyer.

Still seated beside him, Ashley turned toward him. "You were right. Everyone is checking us out as they walk past."

"Yeah. Sorry about that. But they're just curious. Most of them will want to meet you, but they'll leave us alone if we don't approach them. It's a good bunch of people here. They'll respect your boundaries." Most of them thought he was shy, because he tended not to talk much. Little did they know that under most circumstances, he talked more to people here than anywhere else. Except for when he was with Ashley. With her, he couldn't shut up. He didn't know what was with that, but he found it refreshing to just be himself for once.

Ashley glanced to the center aisle, then back to him. "The pastor is coming. It looks like he wants to talk to you."

Sure enough, Pastor Rob had come up from behind the exiting crowd. Instead of following everyone out he turned into the row where Dave and Ashley sat, now alone, and approached them.

Before the pastor spoke, he checked around to make sure

no one was in hearing range. "Hi, Dave. How are you holding up after everything?"

Dave smiled. "Pretty good, thanks for asking. You?"

"Fine. I've missed you for the last couple of weeks. I'm glad you emailed to tell me you were okay." The pastor looked down at Ashley's casted leg, which was propped up on a chair, then back up to Dave's eyes, the question on his face not very subtle.

"It's okay. Pastor Rob, this is Ashley. She's the woman I told you about from the bank when the hostage situation happened." He turned to Ashley. "Pastor doesn't like email, but forces himself to check it once a week."

She smiled at Pastor Rob. "Your church is charming. Thank you for a good message."

The pastor smiled back. "You're more than welcome. Is there anything we can do for you while you're healing? I know Dave is taking care of you, but if you need anything, please don't be shy. We'd love to help you if you need it. Besides it being the Christian thing to do, any friend of Dave's is a friend of ours."

If it wasn't Dave's imagination, he thought Ashley stiffened. "Thanks for the offer. Dave is doing a fine job helping me."

"Great." Pastor Rob turned to Dave. "I need to ask if you'll…" His voice trailed off. "Someone is calling me, I think it's my wife. Please excuse me." He smiled one more time in parting, then turned and walked out of the sanctuary to join everyone in the foyer.

Dave stood, then extended one hand toward Ashley. "It's time we made our way out. I know a lot of people want to meet you. But if you don't want to talk to anyone that's okay. We can go straight home."

Ashley slipped her tiny hand in his and grasped his fingers. "That's okay. I don't mind. Besides, I'd like to meet our mutual friends whose wedding I was supposed to have attended."

He couldn't help but grin. "You did a good job with that in front of the nurses. Even I was starting to think you'd known Tyler and Brittany all your life." He turned and looked at the door leading to the foyer, listening to the murmur of many voices speaking at once. "Tyler and Brittany just got back from their honeymoon late last night, so a lot of people want to talk to them. We'll make it quick and get going."

Even though Dave should have felt more confident, a twinge of nerves bit at him. He could always count on Tyler not to let anything slip into a conversation that shouldn't be there, but by necessity of Tyler getting married, now he also had to trust Brittany. Dave didn't like the widening circle of confidants, especially on a day like today, when Tyler and Brittany were both tired and excited, and also surrounded by a crowd.

It was safer to just leave without talking to them, but he hadn't really talked to his best friend since the day before the robbery. Besides, it would look too strange if he didn't make an appearance, at least for a few minutes.

He helped Ashley stand, then waited while she positioned the crutches to get ready to move. "It's great that your church has chairs instead of pews. I don't know how I could have sat in a pew with this cast, but here all I had to do was move an empty chair to keep my leg elevated. I hadn't thought of that until we got here. I think we should come here every week until things are back to normal."

Part of him wanted exactly that, and part of him was terrified at the thought.

Before he could think too much, Ashley headed for the door, and his friends.

He stayed by her side, then once in the foyer they

headed toward the circle of people surrounding Tyler and Brittany.

As they approached, the crowd parted like the Red Sea.

Tyler's eyes lit up. "Dave!" Tyler stepped forward, wrapped his arms around Dave, and gave him a few manly pats on the back. Tyler lowered his voice to whisper in his ear. "Are you okay?" His voice lowered even more. "Does she know?"

Emotion welled up so fast Dave couldn't speak. All he could do was shake his head.

Tyler released him and stepped back. His eyes flicked to Ashley, then back to Dave, full of questions.

For the first time in a long time, Dave didn't know what to say. He simply cleared his throat, moved so he was standing exactly beside Ashley, and introduced them to each other.

That seemed to be what everyone around them had been waiting for. Before his eyes, everyone in the circle began introducing themselves to her.

Frank, one of the older men, extended one hand as he announced himself. The crowed hushed as Ashley looked down at Frank's hand. He wished he could see her face, but from this angle all he could see was the top of her head and the tip of her nose.

The sudden change in Frank's expression told Dave that Frank had just realized what he'd done. Before he could lower his hand, Ashley leaned her shoulder against Dave, then let go of the crutch with her right hand, and returned the handshake.

Without thinking, as soon as Dave felt her weight against him, he wrapped his arm around her shoulders to support her, maybe both physically, and mentally. At the sight of everyone's widened eyes, he realized what he had just done. In everyone's eyes, he'd just branded them a couple.

Maybe that wasn't such a bad idea.

Pastor Rob appeared next to Tyler, resting one hand on his shoulder. "We've got a little lunch reception about to happen in the meeting room to celebrate our happy couple's return. Very informal. Are you and Ashley staying?"

Dave didn't know much about post-wedding stuff, but it would be a pretty reasonable assumption that the best man should attend something like that. He figured it was also a pretty good guess that the best man's new girlfriend would be expected to attend as well.

He looked down at Ashley at the same time as she looked up at him. "It's up to you," he said. "If you're tired or feel awkward because I'm the only one you know, we don't have to stay. I understand."

She shook her head. "Don't be silly. Tyler is your best friend. I don't mind. We can stay. Lead the way."

With Dave at her side, Ashley followed the crowd to the room where the luncheon was being set up.

Without actually counting the people, she estimated that the youth group at her home church might exceed the head count of the entire congregation here. Of course since she'd never attended any church other than her own she had no idea what normal parameters for a church body might be for an average Sunday service. As a small congregation obviously they wouldn't have the same money to spend on visual aids or sound equipment as her own church. However, this group seemed to rejoice in technology that was at least ten years out of date, or even obsolete. Better or worse, no one seemed to care. She'd seen duct tape on the corner of the overhead projector, and she hadn't seen one of those, in any condition, since elementary school—as a student, not as a teacher.

Yet no one seemed strange or backward. In his sermon, the pastor had suggested what the modern-day applications would be to a few of the parables in the Bible. Then he'd continued by making comparisons between the actions and reactions of the people in the parables to how the same situation would play out in today's world. Unlike at her own church, people in this congregation replied out loud to questions the pastor asked from his sermon, and one man actually stood up and questioned the pastor when there was something he didn't understand.

She hadn't expected it, but here, Dave actually looked comfortable in a crowd. Wearing his baseball cap during a church service would have been disrespectful, but she'd half expected him to not take it off when they walked inside. Yet the second the door closed behind them, the hat was off and stuffed into his back pocket. He'd finger-combed his hair, nodded a greeting to people as they passed, and escorted her into the small sanctuary. Once there he'd turned around an empty chair in front of her to put her leg up, and settled in.

Now, the closer they got to the noise echoing from the room where they were headed, the more the aromas of good food teased her.

What this group didn't spend on equipment, they apparently spent on food.

As they entered the meeting room, Ashley noted they also spent their money on decorating. This wasn't the expected display of streamers and balloons and dollar-store congratulations banners. This room had been professionally decorated to include colored lights and an ice sculpture in the center of the food table. Dave found them seats, including a chair to elevate her leg. As they got her settled the pastor had a few words with Dave, and one of the ladies, whose name she couldn't remember, brought her a cup of coffee.

The room filled quickly, with Tyler and Brittany being the last to enter. When they did everyone greeted them with a round of applause and friendly cheers.

As the applause died down, Dave stood and gave such a warm congratulatory speech it nearly brought tears to Ashley's eyes. When he sat down and she learned that it was completely unrehearsed, her eyes did become moist. Ashley dabbed her eyes with the tip of her napkin, trying to be careful not to smear her mascara. "That was beautiful. You're a very good public speaker."

He shrugged. "This isn't very public. It's just my church."

"You stood in front of people and gave a speech, so that's public enough for me."

"If you say so."

"No. Seriously. You're really good at this. It sounds like you do it all the time."

"I don't. I haven't done a speech in public for five years, and I'm never going to do it again. I'll be right back. Mary looks like she's having trouble with that tray. It's kind of lopsided, and it looks ready to tip."

Before she could point out that someone else was already on their way, Dave rose and jogged to help the lady in distress.

He seemed to be good at that—helping ladies in distress.

She couldn't help but wonder why.

Chapter 10

"How do you feel? Tired? Sore? Overwhelmed?" Dave held his breath, waiting for her reply.

"I'm fine," she muttered as she turned sideways to maneuver the crutches through the doorway.

But she wasn't fine. He could tell by looking at her. It wasn't even lunchtime and already she had dark circles under her eyes.

It took almost everything in him not to pick Ashley up, carry her across the doorway, and deposit her on the couch. But that would be too much like carrying her over the threshold.

Would that really be such a bad thing?

Dave shook his head, then mentally slapped it, too, as he stood back while Ashley aimed herself for the couch and struggled to look brave.

Marriage was not in his future. Like it or not, it was never going to happen.

Now that his best friend had settled into the happily-ever-after, it hit home in a way it never had before. He wanted to imagine the same life that Tyler and Brittany had could also be in store for himself and Ashley. Going to work and coming home to eat dinner together. Maybe go out for the evening, watch another *MythBusters* marathon.

Only if they were married, he wouldn't be going upstairs to go to bed at night.

Now instead of just slapping himself upside the head, he wanted to hit his head against the wall.

He'd only known her for a little over a month. Tyler had known Brittany for two years before he popped the question. The crazy guy was the only one who had any doubt that Brittany would say yes. He could have asked her six months sooner, and the answer would have been the same.

Dave looked at Ashley. The woman was exhausted and drained, and getting cranky. At this stage in a normal relationship, a smart guy would keep his distance and go home to avoid the emotional backlash that was bound to follow. Only he knew what she'd been through, and he wanted to make it all better, even though he knew he couldn't.

As she set the crutches aside on the arm of the couch one wobbled, tottered, then hit the floor.

She only stared at it as it bounced, then lay flat. "Nuts," she muttered, and left it.

Dave hustled across the room, picked it up, and set it up with the other one where she could reach it easily. "The doctor said it was looking good. The X-rays show it's healing really well."

She closed her eyes and sagged into the couch. "He also said it would be another four weeks before the cast comes off. I can't take another four weeks of this. It's heavy, I'm lopsided, it doesn't bend, and it's itchy."

"Yes, but you're getting really good at Scrabble."

"I was already good at Scrabble."

"Maybe, but—"

"Don't start. Quit while you're ahead. Don't you have some work to do?"

He glanced toward the kitchen, where his laptop and a pile of work sat waiting. "Always. Would you like a cup of tea?"

She sighed, let her head drop back along the top of the couch, and covered her eyes with her hands. "No. Thank you. I'm sorry for being cranky. I don't know what I expected. I knew all along it would be between six and eight weeks. I guess I never expected him to say it would take the full eight."

Dave didn't think this was the right time to remind her that the doctor hadn't promised to take the cast off in another four weeks. What he'd said was that in four weeks they would look at it again. For an injury like this, often it was longer.

She sighed again. "You're not saying anything. I know what you're thinking. I know he didn't make any promises. I just want to think it's possible. I think I need a nap. Don't worry about making noise. I'm so tired I think I'll sleep like the dead."

He also didn't think this was a good time to say that the dead didn't sleep. They were…dead.

"Go ahead and get back to work. I know you've got lots to do. Don't let me stop you."

He didn't dare say what he was thinking. He simply turned around and went into the kitchen.

He heard her snoring before he'd finished booting up all the programs he needed. That meant she hadn't rolled over, she'd fallen asleep exactly as he'd left her, sitting on the couch with her head rolled back.

Dave raised his hand and rubbed the back of his own neck. That was going to hurt and she was already in a bad mood. Not that he could blame her. It had been a long morning, ending with news that wasn't very encouraging. And since she hadn't actually been admitted, she'd only been there for an X-ray, they hadn't offered her a wheelchair, and she'd had to make the long journey through the hospital to the X-ray department and then to the specialist's office on the crutches.

But he'd gotten much smarter about going out with her when she was on crutches. Today, just like every day after the first day, he'd brought along a backpack so he could carry her purse and not look like an idiot. He had no idea what she carried that weighed so much. Everything he needed to carry around when he wasn't home fit in his wallet and one pocket. He was smart enough not to ask her to leave the empty purse in the car and transfer the contents to his other pocket and leave what she didn't need that day at home. He simply put the whole purse, unopened, into a backpack, and carried it for her. He couldn't imagine how exhausted she would have been carrying the extra weight of the purse all day. Worse would have been the imbalance of the weight as she tried to carry it while hobbling along on the crutches.

The snoring stopped. Just to make sure she was okay, Dave rose and walked quietly into the living room. She hadn't moved, except her head was now at a very uncomfortable-looking angle.

He couldn't let her stay like that.

He shuffled to her, gently slipped one arm behind her back, cradled her head with the other hand, then lifted and repositioned her so she was lying on her side on the couch. He then lifted her legs to the couch as well, tucked one pillow under her knee, and the smaller pillow under her head. Before he stepped back, he leaned forward and brushed a gentle kiss to her forehead.

How he wanted to kiss her properly when she was awake. But he couldn't. When the cast was off there would be one kiss that was a kiss goodbye, and they would go their separate ways.

Just the thought of it made a lump form in his stomach.

He stood and turned to go back to the kitchen when he heard his backpack ringing.

Normally he wouldn't have answered her phone, but after the morning she'd endured, she needed to sleep. Fortunately for him, she kept her phone tucked in an outside pocket of her purse. He didn't have to open it and violate the woman's code that a man wasn't allowed to see the contents of a woman's purse.

By the middle of the third repeat of her ringtone he had the phone in his hand. He activated the unit and jogged into the kitchen with the phone raised to his ear. "This is Ashley's phone and Dave speaking."

He smiled at the confused pause, then frowned when he heard the voice of Ashley's boss—the principal at the school where she taught. He was less pleased when he heard what the woman wanted. Several teachers were out sick and the principal was in a bind. She needed substitutes and wondered if Ashley could fill in for a couple of days.

"I'm not sure that's a good idea, but I understand the position you're in. I know Ashley misses her students a lot, and I'll ask if she's willing to do that. But only under one condition." He paused to listen for any movement from Ashley. He couldn't say what he needed to if there were any chance Ashley would overhear. For now, she was still sleeping, but his voice would probably wake her if he said much more. He grabbed his keys, then went to finish the conversation outside.

Dave had run upstairs to change, so she still had a couple of minutes.

Ashley straightened her skirt, then hobbled to look at herself in the full length mirror on the closet door.

Part of her was worried to be going back to work, even if for just a couple of days, and another part of her was ecstatic.

She'd been so excited she wanted to call Evan, even though he was at work, but they didn't have time.

A tap sounded on the closed bedroom door. "Are you almost ready? We need to be there as soon as possible."

She glanced at the clock on the night table. He'd been gone barely over five minutes. She didn't know how men did that.

"Almost. Go sit down. I'll be out in a couple of minutes," she called through the door.

Silence on the other side indicated he'd gone to the living room to wait, giving her a chance to check herself one last time. She'd selected the longest skirt she owned, one she hadn't worn for years that she'd found at the bottom of the drawer. As a grade two teacher she'd always worn slacks, but with the cast that was an impossibility.

She smoothed her hair with one hand, then reached to grab the crutches.

After falling asleep on the couch she needed to touch up her makeup. Bad.

Automatically she reached toward the bed for her purse, then remembered it wasn't there. It was still in Dave's backpack, less her phone, in the living room. Fortunately she also had duplicates of everything she needed in the bathroom.

She made good time getting out of the bedroom and down the hall to get to the bathroom. Now that she'd been at it for a month, she'd gotten much more adept on the crutches. If she had to think of anything positive, the muscles on her arms would be quite toned and ready for a rousing tennis tournament. As long as she could stand in one spot on the court.

At the doorway to the bathroom she began to turn, but the bathroom wasn't empty. Dave was inside, and he hadn't closed the door. He stood in front of the mirror leaning toward it, one hand flat on the counter and his head lowered slightly with his eyes focused upward to the top of his head. He raised his other hand and began alternately pressing and tugging at random locks of hair while his eyes narrowed.

His eyes turned to catch her standing there. He straightened abruptly, raised his wrist, and checked his watch. "Are you ready?"

"I need to fix my face."

He looked into her eyes, to her nose, her mouth, gulped, then focused intently back on her eyes. "No ketchup. You're good. Let's go."

"I meant I need to touch up my makeup. Give me a minute."

"That's what you said about getting dressed. You took six minutes."

"Fine. I'll fix it in the car."

The second she'd turned around he strode past her, grabbed the backpack and his baseball cap, and went to the door.

He didn't speak again until they were standing outside his car. He rested his hand on the passenger side door, opened it, then turned to her. "Are you sure you want to do this? It's not too late to change your mind."

Ashley shook her head as she maneuvered herself into the car. "I'm not changing my mind. I want to do this. Besides, even if I do get too tired, it's only for a couple of days. They need me. I'm really glad you agreed to do this. Thank you."

"Don't thank me until it's over," he muttered, and the car door closed.

Chapter 11

"Yay! Miss Kruger!"

The boys began to hoot while most of the girls squealed.

Ashley tried not to beam at her class's enthusiastic response to her return. Even though the reality of it was that school was over for the summer in just two days, she wanted to do a Snoopy Dance because she was back in the classroom. If she could dance.

"Shhhhhh!" Dave cleared his throat, then hunkered down in the middle of the sea of children.

Instantly the class quieted.

At eye level with them, Dave quickly made eye contact with each child individually like he was about to share a very important secret. All the children leaned closer.

With all eyes focused intently on him, Dave finally spoke. He kept his voice barely above a whisper. All the children seemed mesmerized by the deep timbre of his voice and remained hushed. "We're all going to go on tiptoes to our desks and sit down real quietly. Miss Kruger wasn't supposed to come back to school yet, so we had to get permission. The principal is going to be here very soon to make sure she's okay and that we can all take care of her. Mrs. Cartwright has to see everyone sitting very, very quietly doing your reading, but first Miss Kruger is going to tell you something. On the count of three, everyone go up on your tiptoes, and wait. When I say 'now' then tiptoe really slow and very quietly to your desks, fold your hands together, and she can tell you. We need to see how very, very quiet we can be."

Ashley had no idea what she was supposed to tell them that was such an important secret, but she would think of something.

"One."

Most of the children held their breath. A few of the girls covered their mouths with their hands.

"Two." Dave hunched down lower, and some of the children did as well.

He took a deep breath and held it, causing many of the children to do the same.

She could barely stand the suspense when he said, "Three."

All the children and Dave stood, and stretched up all the way to their tiptoes.

Dave raised one finger to his lips. "Shhhh…" The room was so quiet one could hear the proverbial pin drop. "Now," Dave whispered.

In unison, all the children moved like secret spies, tiptoeing quietly and orderly, until all were seated. At the same time, Dave tiptoed to her desk, pulled out her chair, and placed it behind her as she remained balanced on her crutches beside her desk.

She wasn't sure if she was supposed to whisper or not,

but she didn't want to disturb the flow, or the fun everyone seemed to be having with the challenge of being included in a big secret.

Since the chair didn't have arms it would be less than graceful to lower herself into it. While she certainly wasn't about to participate in Field Day, she did need to minimize the difficulty she was having in getting around, between the weight of the cast, and the inability to bend her knee or her ankle.

Instead of sitting, she moved slowly to the desk, then leaned on it like she'd intended to do that all along. Once she felt stable, she removed the crutches and leaned them against the desk.

"Before we do our school work, I'm going to let you all print your names on my cast. But..." she raised one palm in the air to keep them silent "...everyone has to write very, very small so everyone's name can fit. I want everyone to practice printing their name very small, and without a line. If you need help to print it smaller then raise your hand and either Mr. Ducharme or I will come help. Bradley, can you please give everyone one piece of paper?"

Bradley, always the clown, made a great display of tiptoeing around the class, causing a few muffled giggles while he diligently handed one paper to every student.

Suddenly she was very glad that at the last minute she'd slipped on a pair of shorts under her skirt, just in case.

As the class practiced printing their names smaller and smaller, every once in a while some of them looked up at Dave. Always keeping an eye out on the group, Dave returned every look with an encouraging smile.

While the muffled echoes of pencils scratching on the papers filled the room, Ashley watched Dave as he watched the children.

The man was good with children. Not just cautiously good. The man was a natural. She would never have guessed that. Tasha's words came back, with their unspoken warning. She didn't want to believe it was possible that Dave was married, and even more so, that he was married with a family. Or maybe he had a family and he wasn't married, which would explain why he had the freedom to do what he wanted, when he wanted.

The more new things she learned about him, the more she realized she didn't know.

Dave pushed himself away from the wall where he'd perched himself, and approached her. "Are you ready, Miss Kruger?"

That would mean a less than graceful descent into the chair, but she was more than ready. At her nod, Dave helped her sit, then brought a stool to prop her foot. He selected a book and began to read to the class as one by one, the children all took their turn signing her cast.

Just as the last child finished, the principal entered the room.

"Principal Cartwright. It's good to see you," Ashley said.

"I'm so glad you came to help us," Beverley said. "Aren't we, class?"

The class all nodded and murmured their agreement.

"But we have a problem," she said while facing the class, even though Ashley knew Bev was talking to her. "Mr. McNaught has also gotten very sick, and we need to borrow Mr. Ducharme so he can go look after Mr. McNaught's grade five class."

Ashley frowned. The reason she'd been called in on desperate short notice was that before classes started for the day the teachers had participated in a breakfast meeting, and it appeared that something on the menu was tainted. All morning, one by one, everyone who had eaten the eggs had been afflicted with a sudden case of food poisoning. With only two days left in the school year, very few substitute teachers were available, especially after the day had already started, which was why they'd asked if she could come in on an emergency basis.

Bev turned from the students to Ashley. "We've already combined most classes at the same levels, so most of the teachers we have left are looking after two classes, as Mr. McNaught was already doing. Mrs. Wilson's class is already joined up with Mr. McNaught's class. If Mr. Ducharme is unable to take over, we would have to put two combined groups together, meaning one teacher would be looking after four classes alone."

Ashley turned to Dave. Helping to supervise a class of grade two students was a very different from leading a double class of anxious grade fives. But desperate times apparently called for desperate measures. They had no one else who could help on short notice. "I'll be okay. It's up to you."

"Yeah. I can do that," he said, without hesitation. "As long as you're sure."

"I'm sure."

As Dave stood, Ashley's stomach churned, even though their lunch of cafeteria food had been fine. He seemed to be good with children—or at least good with babies. Every time Evan and Karen came over with her two delightful nieces, Dave had shown no hesitation in handling the babies, which she found quite charming. However, this was different. Taking over a group of two combined grade five classes would be hard enough for a seasoned substitute teacher. She couldn't imagine an accountant being thrown in front of such a group.

This late in the year, he couldn't even teach a real lesson out of a textbook. Everything now was basically just filling in time with a group of restless children counting the hours until they were free for summer vacation. It was all ad lib.

He looked at her as if he knew what she was thinking. "I'll be fine. Really." He turned to Bev. "What did you have for breakfast, Principal Cartwright?"

Bev grinned. "Pop-Tarts and coffee. Black. Let's go." She turned back to Ashley. "Thank you both, so much."

The second the door closed, Ashley turned to the class and clapped her hands once. Since she couldn't move very far very fast, she had no leeway to allow any of the children to become restless or distracted. "I'm going to finish reading the book that Mr. Ducharme started, but I'm going to make a change. How would everyone like to take a puppet, and we can act out the story as it happens?"

A rousing cheer assured her that she would keep their interest and maintain control for the remainder of the afternoon.

She knew what to do to occupy a single-class group of seven-year-olds.

She supposed she would find out at the end of the day what an accountant knew about entertaining a double-class of eleven-year-olds.

As worried as she was about Dave, she had no choice but to trust him when he said he would be okay. However, he didn't say he knew what he was doing.

Fortunately the day passed quickly for Ashley. She hoped it had passed quickly for Dave, too.

When the bell rang she wished she could have run to make sure Dave was okay. Instead, she reached for her crutches and once all the children were lined up, escorted them outside in a line to their parents or approved guardians waiting to pick them up. When all from the group whose parents picked them up were gone, the remaining children followed her to the line of buses like chicks behind a mother hen.

Strange, but she'd never before thought about the crowd. How many people were there. How many people she didn't know. How many people looked normal on the surface, but no one knew what problems lay beneath. Or what intent.

No one knew what any of these people carried in their pockets.

Ashley felt herself starting to sweat.

Desperately she searched the crowd—and didn't see Dave. Unfortunately her personal James Bond didn't stand a head above the crowd. He was only average height for a man. She looked again, and still couldn't find him, even though there weren't many men here.

All it took was one.

She tried to tell herself that stuff like that didn't happen at normal elementary schools, but that wasn't true. There had been incidents with crazed gunmen at schools. Maybe more than at banks. As quickly as she could, she shuffled the rest of her class onto the waiting bus, them moved away as the next class started to board.

Waiting beside the last bus in the line was a man with a baseball cap worn low over his face.

She'd found her Ninja warrior. But he was in the middle of a crowd. A crowd full of people she didn't know.

Instead of heading for Dave, Ashley turned and made her way straight to the main entrance of the building. The handicap ramp led away from the door, then back up. It had been fine exiting the building, but to get back in, it was too far to go.

Just like Dave had taught her, she tucked both crutches under her left arm and using the right on the handrail she made her way up the four steps. She quickly positioned the crutches and made her way through the people, who all moved aside as she thumped her way forward, into the building, then to her classroom.

Where she was supposedly safe.

Instead of cleaning up her classroom, Ashley dropped into the armless wooden chair. With shaking hands she rested the crutches against the old desk, then hunched over and covered her face.

This wasn't realistic. Nor was it sensible or practical. She'd been teaching here at this school for five years and there had never been an incident. There had never been even a real worry, only drills, as was required by the school board.

"Ashley? What are you doing? Are you okay?"

Dave sank down to his knees in front of her as she lowered her hands.

A foolish tear dribbled down her cheek. "What's wrong with me? Why do I feel this way? Nothing is going to happen. The risk of something happening is very small. But every time I looked around I didn't see friends or coworkers. I saw potential threats and crazy people. I was so scared I couldn't even stand around and talk. I had to come back inside. Am I losing it?"

Dave pulled off his cap, shoved it into his back pocket, then picked up her hands and gave them a gentle squeeze. "How you feel is normal. I also know you're going to struggle with this for a long time. If you want, talking to Pastor Rob can help. He's got a lot of good things to say. He can help you work it out and then he'll pray with you, and keep praying for you." Dave paused. "What do you think? I can call him and you can probably even meet with him tonight."

Ashley looked into his eyes. She couldn't help but wonder how Dave knew this.

Dave stood. "I don't have to clean up the classroom. I made the kids do it. Let me help pick up in here, and we'll go home."

"You made them clean up?"

He shrugged as he began to pick up a few stray puppets and put them in the box. "Not really. I kind of made them think they were offering."

"What did you do with forty kids all afternoon?"

He turned and grinned over his shoulder. "What do you think? Math. Now let's go home. I worked up a good appetite, and we have some great leftovers in the fridge."

Chapter 12

Echoes of some movie drifted from the living room to the kitchen while Dave struggled to keep his mind on his work.

He'd sat and chatted with Pastor Rob's wife while the pastor had taken Ashley into his home office to talk.

Ashley had come out with red, puffy eyes and hadn't said a word the whole way home.

Home. Funny how he'd come to think of her small apartment as home. He didn't even consider his own apartment where he'd lived for four years to be home, much less the mattress on the floor in the suite above. But in less than five weeks, he'd started to feel that when he walked in through Ashley's door, he was putting down roots.

This wasn't good.

In order not to dwell on it, he put his mind back on his work.

Just as he hit Save, he heard Ashley blowing her nose.

He lowered his head, pressed his knuckles to his forehead, and sighed deeply. He remembered the first time he'd had a heart-to-heart with Pastor Rob. While he'd felt pulled through an emotional wringer, instead of falling to pieces he'd started the path to putting his life back together, and feeling better. Ashley was supposed to feel better, too, or else he wouldn't have suggested she do the same.

He didn't know anything about crying women. However he did know a little about getting shot.

He stood, automatically pressed his palm to his left shoulder, stiffened, then walked into the living room.

Ashley reached into the box of tissues beside her, dabbed at her eyes, blew her nose again, and dropped the used tissue onto a pile of already used tissues beside the box.

Dave didn't have a good feeling about this. He knew that the emotional recovery was often more difficult than the physical. Sometimes those emotional wounds never healed.

When she saw him coming she swiped at her eyes with the back of her hand, sniffled, then pasted on a smile that even he knew was fake.

He sat close beside her, knowing she wasn't likely to move away, and held her hands in his. On the television, the credits rolled by.

"Wanna talk?" Being a woman, she probably needed to talk out her feelings to straighten them out, without necessarily needing or even wanting him to say anything or offer suggestions. If that was what she wanted, he could be a great listener.

She sniffled again. "Watching *Fly Away Home* always makes me cry. I don't know why. I know what's going to happen."

"How many times have you watched it?"

"I don't know. Dozens of times, at least. I love watching the baby geese grow up to make their flight of triumph." She sniffled again. "This was my favorite movie when I was a little girl. It probably still is. I love all animal movies. I even love *Lady and the Tramp,* and that makes me cry, too, even though it's a cartoon."

"Why do you watch movies that you know are going to make you sad?"

She sniffled and blew her nose again. "I'm not sad."

"But you're crying."

She swiped at her eyes with her sleeve. "No, silly, these are happy tears."

He'd never thought of tears as happy. But far be it for him to discredit a crying woman.

"You're not saying anything. You don't believe me, do you?"

"Uh…sure. I don't understand you, but I believe you."

"Would you like to watch the movie with me?"

"But you just saw it."

"So?"

Dave couldn't make sense of this. First she liked watching a movie she'd seen multiple times already, second it made her cry. And now she wanted to watch it again?

He reminded himself—he was not going to discredit a crying woman. "Sure. I'll watch it with you. Want me to make popcorn?"

Ashley dug into the popcorn bowl with one hand and pointed to the screen with the other. "Watch the little baby goose on the left. See what it does?"

"It's waddling. Like a goose."

"But isn't it cute?"

"I've never thought of geese as cute." Even as he dissed her sentiments, he smiled at the adorable group of goslings.

She turned back to watch the movie. Ashley couldn't believe the emotional roller coaster she'd traveled on today, and she still hadn't disembarked.

After all the tension of the day, watching a movie that made her cry had been such a release that she wanted, even needed, to watch it again.

Men never understood that. When it happened, instead of lending a shoulder for a woman to cry on, most men left faster than if they were being chased by a rabid grizzly bear.

But not Dave. Here he was, knowing she was going to cry before the movie ended, still sticking around for the fallout.

It was one more reason she felt herself falling in love with him. Yet, for all the good things about him that would make any woman fall head over heels for a man like him, she couldn't do this.

Despite his good qualities, he was taking extreme measures to hide something important—and that was something she couldn't live with.

She didn't want to compare him to her father and all his deceit, but the withholding of something so very important and life-changing as being shot made his truth into a lie. If it was accidental, or a hunting accident, while that would still be horrible, it was nothing to hide.

He was hiding both being shot, and the reason for it. Hiding the truth made him a liar.

She could never fall in love with a liar.

She'd tried to find out from Pastor Rob what Dave had been involved in, but the pastor had pointedly changed the subject every time she pushed it. This told her Pastor Rob knew what had happened. Using his Pastor Code Of Confidentiality, he not only wouldn't give her even a hint of what had happened, he changed the subject so fast her head spun.

A pastor's job was to be like God and forgive anyone for anything and everything. Even if Dave confessed what he'd done to God, and to Pastor Rob, he was still keeping it a secret from everyone else, and her.

She hoped it wasn't the same kind of secret as her father's. If it was, Ashley couldn't live with that. In her heart she hadn't been able to forgive her father for being the cause of her mother's death. He'd cheated on his wife—and he'd had another family on the side. Nor had she been able to forgive him for selling the house out from under them and leaving them on the street to fend for themselves the day they turned eighteen. They were still in high school, and even though they were adults in the eyes of the law, they had no way to support themselves unless they dropped out of school. Her father had never asked them for forgiveness, not then, and they hadn't seen or heard from him since the day he gave them their notice to leave the house. After he sold the house out from under them he simply disappeared, which meant he wasn't asking for forgiveness. He wanted his freedom, and he got it.

He'd been good at hiding his other family. He also had to have been hiding parts of his income in order to have lives in two different homes. He'd been good at covering his tracks.

Dave was also covering his tracks. Besides hiding his face every time he went out in public, which she'd learned he didn't do often, now she'd discovered that he dyed his hair, which would be for the benefit of anyone who saw him without his nearly always present ball cap.

As Dave watched Amy and her father scramble with the geese, Ashley watched Dave.

What was he hiding?

Trust was the basis for any relationship. Without trust, there was no foundation.

Yet he'd done some rather extreme things to get her to trust him. She had a copy of his driver's license, which for all he knew she'd already turned in to the police, in case something happened to her. She knew where he lived, and where he worked. She'd also written down his license plate numbers and given them to Natasha. She knew where he went to church, and she'd met his best friend, who seemed like a really nice guy.

These were not the actions of a man with a nefarious background.

He turned and looked at her. "You were right. This movie is really good. Even though the ending has to be that they succeed and get the geese to fly south, I still want to watch it. I like stuff with a happy ending." He turned back to the television and sighed, except he sounded so sad instead of happy.

She wanted to ask him if maybe he thought he'd never have a happy ending, but she didn't want to ruin the evening for him.

"Then you'll really like the end of this."

Sure enough, by the time Amy flew past the office tower with the geese, tears were already burning her eyes.

All it took was for Dave to look at her and they burst out.

"What? I..." he stammered, looking very helpless. "Why are you crying? They're on their way, look at all the support they've got. They're going to make it. This isn't sad."

He stared into her face. She couldn't tell if he was confused, terrified, or a mixture of both. "Do you want to watch the rest of the movie?" He reached for the remote.

She sniffled, then nodded. "Of course."

As they settled in to watch the rest of the movie, which she probably knew by memory from this point, Dave slowly reached toward her and rested his hand gently on her shoulder. Because it seemed like a normal and natural thing to do, she leaned toward him. Completing the motion, his hand slipped over her shoulder, causing her to lean into him with his arm around her. She snuggled in, as if it were the most natural thing to do. She wanted to make a comment about teenaged boys taking a girl to a scary movie to do this very thing, but as she started to open her mouth to speak, he rested his cheek to the top of her head and sighed. For a few seconds, he held her tighter, then relaxed just a bit.

They settled in to watch the rest of the movie in silence, except for the sounds of Ashley sniffling.

She almost didn't want to disturb the moment, but just as Amy landed, Ashley reached the point that she couldn't breathe, and she really needed to blow her nose.

Of course as she leaned forward to pull a tissue from the box she moved completely out of Dave's embrace.

She immediately felt cold.

Diligently, she blew her nose, which only helped marginally. She turned her head to make a joke about blubbering like an idiot, but when she turned toward him, he reached up and brushed the tears away from her cheeks with his thumbs. Instead of pulling away, he slid his knuckles lightly down her cheeks and cradled her chin in his palms.

His voice came out low, and soft. "I don't think I've told you how beautiful you are."

She wasn't the least bit beautiful. She'd cried all her

makeup off, her eyes were red and puffy, her skin would be blotchy, and her nose probably rivaled Rudolph's, plus it was shiny and dripping, which was pretty disgusting.

The classy thing to do would be to push away, stand up to give herself some distance, then go to the bathroom and shut the door to clean herself up.

Except she couldn't stand without making an issue of it.

"I want to kiss you, but that's probably not a good idea."

She shook her head frantically enough for him to drop his hands. "No. Not a good idea. I can't breathe. I have to blow my nose. Properly this time."

As the music and credits rolled through, Ashley struggled to push herself up. Dave handed her the crutches, allowing her to hobble off to the bathroom.

Not dignified, but it worked.

After she closed the door, she sat on the closed toilet, lifted her casted leg to rest on the edge of the tub, plunked her elbows on her knees, and leaned forward to cover her face with her hands.

She'd wanted to kiss him.

She'd liked that he wanted to kiss her.

If she could breathe through her nose, she probably would have kissed him.

It was probably the worst decision of her life. She knew a lot about him, but there was too much she didn't know.

He was sweet, kind, and helpful to a fault. But he'd done something that caused him to hide—something horrible enough that he'd been shot and wasn't going to talk about it.

She didn't know what to do.

A tap sounded on the door. "Are you okay in there? We both have to get up early, so I'm going to head back to my place upstairs. I'll see you in the morning."

* * *

Dave waited for the last of his class to get on the bus, then stepped back. Out of the corner of his eye he watched Ashley hustle back into the building, at least as much as she could hustle. He almost turned to follow her, but a few of the girls waved at him as the bus began to pull away. He stopped, pushed up the brim of his cap, waved back, and stayed still, watching them go until the bus disappeared in the distance.

He couldn't believe how he felt. He hadn't been all that affected last night by a movie designed to be a tear jerker. But now, as he waved goodbye to a group of kids he'd only known for two days and would probably never see again, he felt like he'd been kicked in the solar plexus.

"Hard to say goodbye, isn't it?"

He looked to his side and down to see the principal standing beside him. "Yeah. I didn't know it would be like this." He didn't want to say how he used to feel on the last day of school. He'd probably already told her too much, but being a principal, Bev knew how to keep things confidential, and so he trusted her. Besides, she'd accepted his terms on everything he'd demanded in order for him to do the job she so desperately needed.

If only he could tell Ashley. But his circle of "need to know" had already expanded too much. He couldn't risk adding another.

"They loved you, and I can't believe you actually taught them something on the last day of school when they were itching to be out the door. If you're ever looking for another job, let me know."

"You know I can't do that."

Bev nodded. "I know. I just had to say it, in case something changes."

It wasn't going to change. At least not that he could see in the next two decades.

The longer time went on, the harder this became, when he'd thought it would get easier. This meant it was time again to remind himself why he was doing this, and what was at stake. Automatically he pressed his hand to his shoulder.

His reminder was in his wallet, but he couldn't look at it here—where he needed to be silent and put on a happy face…for those who could see his face.

As the saying went, a picture told a thousand words, even though all he needed was one. Tonight, he would take the time and look at that picture again, to justify what his life had become.

He turned to Bev, again pulling the brim of the cap down. "I think I need to take Ashley home. It was nice meeting you. Maybe I'll see you again in twenty years."

Chapter 13

The echo of a gunshot blasted through her consciousness.

Ashley jolted awake, sitting up with a start.

As she gasped for air, the world drifted into focus.

It had been a dream. Another one.

This time she'd been at the mall, alone, walking around, no crutches, no cast, no broken leg. She'd just started to open her wallet to pay for a new pair of jeans when a shot fired. She'd felt the pain in her leg all over again, except this time the noise had woken her up.

She'd heard about people having recurring nightmares after a traumatic event. Maybe unrealistically, she'd thought they would fade. But they hadn't. It had been five weeks now, and even though they weren't every night, she'd had many.

She'd seen Dave have a nightmare the day he'd brought her home from the hospital. She didn't know the circumstances of how he'd been shot, but she'd concluded it had been years ago. She didn't know how often he had the nightmares, but she would ask him. Although, if he still had them, asking him how to make them stop was a question he obviously couldn't answer.

The bang sounded again, only this time it wasn't the resounding explosion of a gun—it was a knock at her door.

Her whole body went into alert. Even if she sleep-walked, she couldn't have done so with the cast. She hadn't pressed the button to open the main door to let anyone in.

The clock showed Dave had only been gone half an hour. He wouldn't be returning for another hour. When he left he knew she would be sleeping, and had said he'd use his key and let himself in.

Someone was out there—someone who had bypassed the security of the front door. Dave wasn't here to save her. She was pretty sure he'd locked the door to her apartment when he left, but she couldn't get up fast enough to check for sure.

The knock sounded again. "Ashley? Are you home? It's me. Steve."

The pounding of her heart began to slow, but at the same time, her teeth clenched. She hadn't seen Steve since their last date, which was also the last time she'd ever wanted to see him again.

He pounded yet again. "I know you're home. I asked Mrs. Beasley and she let me in. I heard what happened and I just want to talk. I'm worried about you."

Ashley sighed. So that's how he'd gained entrance to the building. Steve's most endearing trait, and the most un-endearing, was how he could convince almost anyone of almost anything. Unfortunately, for too long, that had included herself.

That was also what made him a good lawyer.

Someone who defended the guilty, and won on technicalities, for money.

At first she'd thought he was a noble person, helping innocent people defend themselves. But as she got to know him better she learned that the cases he was the most proud of winning were not those where he defended the downtrodden. His favorite clients, and cases, were very wealthy people who hired him and paid him well to clean up after them. Drunken driving cases where innocent people were injured, or even killed. Assault cases that were not self-defense. A few messy divorces.

He'd even done a bit of ambulance chasing.

After she learned his true colors, Ashley wanted no part of a person like that. While the world did have many good and righteous lawyers defending the innocent, Steve wasn't one of them.

When they first started dating she'd thought he was proud of her being an elementary school teacher. However, she later learned that he'd considered her merely an educated babysitter. He'd seen her as little more than arm candy, a dumb blonde on the arm of the sophisticated and dashing lawyer. She also suspected that he only had gone to church with her because it looked good and made him appear like he had morals.

"I'm fine, and I was having a nap. You can go now."

"I know you're not fine. I heard you were shot at that bank robbery. Besides, I've got something for you."

It was probably childish to have their conversation through the door, but Ashley had no desire to see Steve in person. "I don't need anything from you. I don't want your gifts."

He cleared his throat. "It's not a gift. I found your red hat and I want to return it to you."

Ashley's breath caught. Her mother had knitted her that hat—it was the last thing she had left that her mother had made for her. Steve had always hated that hat. When she couldn't find it she'd feared Steve had thrown it out. In fact, an argument over the hat being tacky was the first thing that had opened her eyes to Steve's true colors.

He said because she was blonde, wearing red made her look like a cheap hooker.

She'd later learned that an expensive hooker would have been okay with him. He defended those too, because they could pay enough for his services and he didn't care where the money came from.

She couldn't believe she'd been so naive, believing all his justification that he was truly doing the right things, hiding the dirty details until she started putting all the pieces together to make a very ugly picture.

As much as she didn't want to see Steve ever again, she did want her hat back.

"Hold on. I'm coming."

She'd intended to just take the hat and dismiss him, but when she opened the door his reaction caught her off guard. His shocked expression at her cast and that she was balancing on crutches made her pause, which gave him enough time to walk in, like he'd been invited. Which he hadn't.

He sat on one end of the couch, glanced around her clean living room, and frowned. "Are you able to take care of yourself? I see you've hired someone to clean your place. I hope you're not paying too much."

Ashley remained standing. Or at least leaning on the crutches. "No, a friend is doing my housekeeping."

He looked at the empty Chinese food container on the coffee table. "I see you're doing takeout for your meals. Are you eating okay?"

"I'm doing fine. Actually, it's been a long time since I've had takeout. A friend is cooking for me. He just picked this up because he had someplace else to be this evening."

"He? You mean a man bought your dinner today? Are you dating?"

Ashley opened her mouth, but no words came out. Despite the amount of time she and Dave spent together, there was no real relationship. He'd been clear about his plans to help her until she was back on her feet, but he'd given her no indications of his intent after that. She hoped they would continue to be friends, but she really didn't know.

"No. We're not dating."

Steve leaned forward. "That's good that you haven't involved yourself with someone else. I wanted to talk to you tonight. When I heard what happened, I just felt sick. I feel bad about the way things ended between us, and when I was told you'd been shot it made me realize how much I still care for you. What I'm asking is if you'll give me another chance."

Something inside her softened. Just a little. Not enough to reconsider. While she believed a person could reform, she didn't believe that was Steve's intent. "I'm sorry, I'm touched that you feel that way, but I don't think it would work between us."

"Then let me help you."

"Help me? I don't need any help." Dave was going out of his way to do everything she needed, and then some.

Steve ran his fingers through his hair. "You know I'm a good lawyer."

All she could do was stare at him. No flies on this guy.

"You don't have to suffer while you're laid up, you know. The bank should be paying for this. They have lots of money. They should be giving you compensation."

"They are. They offered to pay my medical bills, which I thought was fair. It's not their fault they were robbed."

His face tightened. "Actually, it is. They didn't have adequate security, and I can prove it. And when I do, you'll get a good settlement to take care of your added expenses while you're unable to work, and you'll also get compensation for pain and suffering. All we need to do is find the guy who took the robber down to prove that the security was sadly lacking."

"Leave him out of this."

Steve shrugged his shoulders. "Fine. We don't really need him anyway. Everything we need will be on video."

Ashley leaned against the wall. This was starting to sound even uglier. She wanted to distance herself from what happened, not bury herself in the details of it, over and over. "I'm not going to sue the bank. I'm doing fine."

"Banks have funds set up for this. I can help you get what's due to you."

Visions of her bank balance danced through her head, and the vision wasn't the happy sugar plums of Christmas lore.

While all of her medical bills were covered, and she did receive some wage loss benefits, she was taking a big hit financially. The full impact hadn't hit her yet because she had some savings, but she was only halfway through the expected recovery period, and she didn't know how much physical therapy she'd need, or for how long it would last.

She did expect to be back teaching full-time when the new school year started, but she had no guarantees.

She didn't know what to do.

"Let me think about it." She glanced to the clock. She didn't want him here, but soon Dave would be back, and that would get him to leave. Then she could think.

"You're looking at the clock. I should probably leave."

True to his word, he stood. But instead of leaving, he approached her. Since she needed her hands to support herself on the crutches she was helpless to slap his hand away when he brushed a lock of hair out of her face. "I've really missed you. I've also realized a lot of the things you said were right. I'm trying to change that."

Without saying any more, he turned and left.

But his words remained.

"We need to talk."

Inwardly, Dave cringed. He didn't know much about women, but he did know that phrase meant something ominous.

He forced himself to smile, and hoped it didn't look as fake as it felt. "Sure. What's up?"

"Do you remember I told you that I'd recently broken up with a man, and he was a lawyer?"

"Yes." He remembered. She hadn't told him any details beyond that, and he hadn't asked for more because he couldn't give her any details from his own pathetic life.

"He paid me a surprise visit while you were gone."

Dave joined her on the couch, sitting beside her, afraid to touch her, but strangely afraid not to. Because it was the least invasive, he picked up one of her hands and began massaging her wrist with his thumb. "What happened? He didn't hurt you, did he?" If the man had hurt her, he didn't know what he would do, but he feared it wouldn't be pretty.

Ashley shook her head. "No, of course not, but he said some stuff." She gulped. "To make a long story short, he said I should sue the bank."

Dave blinked. "Why? You told me they paid for your medical expenses. Did they renege?"

"No. But he says they owe me more. He says they should also pay me for pain and suffering, and loss of income. I'm really confused. I don't know what to do."

"The first thing you should do is pray about it."

"Of course."

Dave also needed to pray about this. If it was a legitimate lawsuit, he couldn't in good conscience discourage Ashley from following through. Yet, he didn't think it was right. The bank had quickly offered to pay for her medical expenses, but as to more, it wasn't their fault they'd been robbed, so he didn't think they owed her more. As far as he'd seen, they had adequate security measures in place. As unfair as it seemed, it was a fact of life that bad things happened, and all they could do was make the best of it.

Rather than the bank, her injury was his fault. If he hadn't fought the robber, Ashley would have been kidnapped. They both had come to the same conclusion as to the outcome of that, which was that she would probably have been killed before she could escape or was released. A broken leg was by far the lesser of those two evils. Of course that was supposition, but he hadn't wanted to take the risk that someone would be killed if there was something he could do to prevent it. Ashley felt the same way, and wasn't holding him responsible for being shot, even though he knew he was.

Thinking back to the reason for Steve's visit, Dave had to wonder why it took Steve five weeks to suggest that Ashley sue the bank. Dave doubted this was the first he had heard about it. After all, they had to travel in some of the same circles, or they never would have met. That said, Dave thought it more likely it had taken this long to do his research on the legalities of suing the bank, and the likelihood of success.

He'd never heard of anyone suing a bank for personal injury after a robbery, but that wasn't to say it had never happened. On the other side, he hadn't been impressed with some of the things Ashley had said about Steve—his lack of honorable ethics had been the reason she broke off with him. In his heart he suspected this was another form of ambulance chasing. That said, people could change, and they could repent.

He would have to check this guy out. Later. For now, the ball was in Ashley's court. Ultimately, whichever way she went, it was her decision, and he didn't want to influence her.

They remained seated on the couch while they prayed together. When they were done Ashley raised her head and looked at him before he could stand. "I know you won't have to go to court over the bank robbery, but if me suing the bank goes to court, you'll probably have to testify. Would you do that?"

Dave's stomach churned. A case like that would immediately be made public. Very public. Automatically he reached back and put his hand over the pocket containing his wallet, and the photo. "No."

He could see the question "why" in her eyes, but she didn't ask it. And he didn't answer.

Instead of testifying he could simply disappear. Then the courts would be forced to use the video of the bank robbery as their evidence of the chain of events.

He didn't want to put his life through that again, but if Ashley did decide to sue the bank, he wouldn't stop her. Because he loved her. He hadn't known her long, but they'd spent almost all their waking hours together since she'd been released from the hospital. He would do that for her, if that was the way it had to be.

He grasped her tender hands and gave them a gentle

squeeze, looking down at them because he couldn't look at her face. "If you feel suing the bank is what you need to do, then do it. You should probably talk to Steve again to see what it entails."

Ashley pulled her hands out from his, and he let her go. He'd expected her to straighten and push him away, but instead her hands rose toward his face and she cupped his chin, pushing his chin up, not releasing his cheeks and forcing him to look at her.

"I probably won't. We had an agreement, and they've done exactly what they said they would do without complaint. Also, I have a feeling that if I did, I'd never see you again. Why won't you tell me why you're hiding, or from whom? Is what you've done that bad?"

He gulped. If he had to explain, that would open doors that needed to stay closed. He couldn't drag her in more than he'd already done. The risk was too great.

Dave leaned back, forcing her to release him, and stood. "Yes," he said simply, turned and walked out.

Chapter 14

To say the relationship between them had become strained was an understatement.

Now, if Ashley found out what he was doing, it would be even worse.

He trusted Ashley to do the right thing. However, she could only make her decision based on the facts she'd been given. If she was given incorrect or misleading information, then she couldn't be responsible for a choice that could be life-altering.

That was one thing he knew about, having to make a life-altering choice.

He'd made an appointment with Steve at his office. Not knowing how bad the traffic would be he arrived quite early. Rather than wait in the car, he went into the office half an hour early, hoping for the best.

When he identified himself and stated the time of his appointment, the receptionist looked down to the clock on her desk. "I'm so sorry, Mr. Wasenforth has been held up in court. I tried to call you but there was no answer."

Dave reached into his pocket to find out the hard way that the battery on his cell phone had died.

She looked up at him. "Can we rebook?" She flipped the pages in her appointment calendar. "How about next Tuesday at 10:30? Or if you want, I can squeeze you in for a short time before his first appointment after lunch today."

He tried to smile politely. "Yes, I'd prefer that." Next week would be too late. He needed to talk to Steve before he talked to Ashley. Only now he had over an hour to kill downtown. Checking his watch, he considered his options. He didn't want to walk around the streets. In the suburbs the ball cap and sunglasses were ordinary, but here, in the expensive section of downtown, most of the men on the street wore suits and ties and carried a laptop case with one hand, while talking on the phone with the other. Here, the ball cap and large sunglasses would draw attention instead of deflecting it.

He considered staying here and reading out-of-date magazines three times each.

Perhaps the receptionist sensed his unease. She gave him a professional smile and slid a piece of paper across the desk. "I'm really sorry. I can assure this doesn't happen often. I'd like to give you a coupon for a latte, on us, at the coffee shop downstairs, while you're waiting. They also have really good club sandwiches. All of us eat there often, not just because it's close. The food is really good."

Dave considered himself dismissed, so he picked up the coupon and made his way to the door. Before he left, since he had nothing better to do, he stopped to check a collage of framed photos on the wall.

Prominently displayed were labeled photographs of

many of the lawyers from the office. He searched for a picture of the infamous Steve.

Sure enough, there was a photo of Steve shaking hands with the mayor as the mayor handed him a certificate. For the shot, Steve and the mayor both smiled brightly for the camera.

Steve was a handsome man—tall, blond, and confident. Knowing only a little about him, the photo fit Ashley's description of him—arrogant and able to talk a bee out of his honey. Visually, he and Ashley would have made a good-looking couple. Looks aside, from the few things she'd said of him, Dave knew Ashley and Steve were as opposite as night and day.

On the other hand, Dave and Ashley would make good life partners. Soul mates even. They shared so much in common, and she was even a teacher. But that was not to be.

He took one last look, slipped the coupon in his pocket, and left the room.

Once at the coffee shop, Dave placed his order, then turned to find an empty seat.

Just like a cop, he wanted to find a table where he could watch the door, although he didn't feel the need to have his back to a wall.

As he stood waiting for a couple that looked like they were about to stand, two men in suits entered.

One let out a boisterous laugh and slapped the other on the back.

Dave froze. He stood in one spot while Steve and his companion ordered their lunches.

Instead of waiting for a table, the two men sat on stools at the counter.

Dave couldn't pass up this opportunity. He walked to the counter, and lowered himself to the stool beside them.

"Number 367!" the server called out.

Dave raised his hand, and his meal was served.

He ate slowly. Very slowly. And listened to the conversation beside him.

As they waited for their order Steve rubbed his hands together, then picked up his mug and blew across the hot surface of his latte. "You think that was an attention grabber, just wait until you see what I've got in the works."

The other man grunted as he sipped his coffee. "What?"

"Remember that bank robbery just over a month ago, when some moron attacked an armed robber who was holding him and a woman hostage and was making a break for Mexico?"

The man nodded. "Yeah. It was in all the papers. The guy disappeared, right in the middle of everything. Great police system we've got, losing a key witness."

"I've got an in on that one. I know the woman who was taken hostage and shot. She's my ex." The glee in Steve's voice sang out, almost to the point of sarcasm.

The other man returned his cup to the saucer with a clink. "Really?"

"Really. I saw her last night. I almost have her convinced to sue the bank."

"Is that so?"

Steve nodded. "Think of what the media circus can do for us. The little guy winning against corporate America. She's going to sue the bank for pain and suffering. Remember, the gunman shot her in the leg."

"That's gotta hurt. Still, what if you don't win?"

Steve laughed outright. "I'll win. If I'm not getting what I want on pain and suffering I'm going to go on mental instability caused by the robbery. Remember, I used to go with her, and we were pretty solid for a while. I know exactly what buttons to push."

Dave nearly choked on his sandwich, causing both men to look at him as he stifled his cough.

"Number 372!" the server called out.

The man with Steve raised his hand.

It didn't surprise Dave that Steve hadn't paid for the meal.

"I have a feeling she knows who the guy is who took down the armed robber. The guy no one can find. We can subpoena her, then she'll have to tell us where to find him. Think of the recognition we'll get for pulling him out into the media." He rubbed his hands together. "Once the furor dies down, then we can get her to sue him too. After all, he's the reason she got shot. Reckless endangerment."

This time Dave did choke on his sandwich.

Steve pushed his glass of water toward him. "Here buddy. You gonna be okay?"

Dave nodded as he sipped the water. "Yeah. Thanks," he muttered, deposited the rest of his uneaten sandwich on the plate, tossed a tip on the counter, walked to the elevator, and pushed the button to go to the underground parking.

Once in his car he plugged his cell phone into the adapter outlet, and called Steve's office.

"I'd like to cancel my appointment. It's no longer needed. No, I do not wish to rebook. Thank you."

He drove to Ashley's apartment on autopilot. He was almost there when his phone rang. He wasn't in the mood to talk, but the hands-free Bluetooth system kicked in and answered it.

He didn't say anything. If it was a wrong number the person would hang up.

"Dave? You there? It's me, Tyler."

Dave sighed. "I'm in the car and I don't really feel like talking right now. Is this important?"

"You've got trouble. Ashley just phoned me. I don't know what's going on, but she asked a lot of questions about you. Background stuff. How long I've known you. And if I know what kind of trouble you're in. I don't know what you did, but for some reason she sounded really mad. I thought you should know. Good luck. Bye."

So that he wouldn't have an accident, Dave pulled over. When the car was at a full stop, he turned it off, grasped the top of the steering wheel, then slumped and let his forehead rest on his fingers.

He'd prayed this day wouldn't come, but it had.

He'd gotten in too deep with her. He had two choices, neither of them good. He could tell her everything, or tell her nothing.

Either way he would have to face her wrath.

Either way, he might have to start his life all over again…again.

Dave turned the ignition and headed home. For however long it could be his home.

The time had finally come, and there was no turning back.

Ashley didn't know where he'd gone, but it wasn't work. His boss had called to ask why he wasn't answering his cell.

As if she would know.

Following that, she'd also called, and gone to voicemail.

The mystery of Dave continued.

After his boss called she'd called his friend to ask why

his boss was so concerned. Tyler gave her the runaround and wouldn't answer a single one of her questions.

Both men knew what Dave wasn't telling her, and neither of them would tell her, either.

At the same time, Tyler had sounded concerned that Dave wasn't answering his phone as well.

As if she wasn't worried already, now she was even worse.

If she had been able to pace, she would be doing that right now.

Rather than sit, she pushed herself up and made her way to the window, watching for Dave's car.

She didn't know what kind of trouble he was in, but the secrets were driving her insane. With the reappearance of Steve, even though asking for help was the last thing she wanted to do, maybe she could ask to send Dave to the right people who could do something.

She stared out the window for a few more minutes, and was just about ready to call the police when Dave's car appeared down the street. She watched every movement as he parked, left the car, and jogged to the door. She'd only made it halfway across the room when his knock sounded through her apartment door. "Ashley? It's me. Dave. Are you there?"

"Of course I'm here. Come in."

If only she could cross her arms. The best she could do was glare at him as he walked in the door. She opened her mouth to chastise him for worrying everyone, but stopped short.

"You look awful. What's wrong?" Not that she expected him to tell her. After all, he hadn't told her anything so far.

He looked directly into her eyes, telling her that whatever it was, it was bad.

"We have a problem. We need to talk."

He waited for her to get to the couch, then sat beside her without going into the kitchen to make coffee first.

This was really bad.

He sucked in a deep breath. "I made an appointment to see Steve today."

"What?" Ashley clenched her teeth. "Why?"

"After what you said, I wanted to ask him how exactly he thought he could sue the bank, especially since they've done everything they said they would with your medical bills."

"I was planning on asking him that, you know." Unless Dave was planning on giving some information that apparently everyone around her knew, and she still didn't. The more she thought about it, he should never have been left alone with one class of children at the school, much less two. He had to have told Bev something in order for her to leave Dave in charge, without supervision.

Even her boss knew more about Dave than she did.

Why was she the only one who didn't know?

"I know you were going to talk to Steve. Honestly, from what you said about him, I thought he would speak more openly to me as a man, than to you. As well, I thought doing it at his office would make him think he had a psychological advantage, and he'd reveal more."

She crossed her arms over her chest. She was getting a real bad feeling about this. "Continue."

"I never made it to his office. Well, I sort of did. When I got there they said they'd tried to phone to cancel, but the battery on my cell died and I never got the call."

"Ya think, Sherlock?" she muttered.

He sighed. "I went for lunch to kill time while I waited for him, and he walked into the coffee shop. His picture was on the office wall, so I knew what he looked like, but he didn't know who I was. I listened in on a very interesting conversation."

As Dave relayed what he'd heard, Ashley felt her face getting hotter and hotter. "Reckless endangerment? But you saved my life! That guy had lost it. He had a gun and nothing to lose. I know he would have killed me once we got to Mexico!"

Dave raised his palms toward her. "You don't have to yell. I know that." His hands lowered to his lap. "Still, that doesn't lessen the fact that I was responsible for you getting shot. I should have slammed his wrist harder into the floor. I should have hit harder to get him to drop the gun when I took him down, and that didn't happen."

"It was something no one could have predicted. In the end, I'm not that seriously hurt. In the big picture of a lifetime, this is just a blip." She shrugged as some of the anger drained away. If it hadn't happened, she would never have met Dave, and looking back, that would have been worse. "Who knows, maybe one day I'll write a book about this."

Instead of laughing, Dave's face paled and he shrank back in the chair. "What do you mean?"

The moment she said it, she realized she'd made a mistake. "Nothing. It was just a joke." She sighed. "The more I think about this, the madder I get. I think I'm just trying to reduce the tension. I could never write a book. I can barely write a grocery list."

She waited for him to agree since he'd seen what was in her cupboards before he took over in the kitchen, but he didn't.

"Tonight I'll call and tell him I know what he was planning. There is no way I'm going to let him make a fool of me or have me declared mentally incompetent in court. Do you know what that would do to my job? I'd be put on permanent medical leave. They'd never allow a teacher who was deemed unstable to teach children."

Dave nodded. "That's true."

The more she thought about it, the angrier she became. "He was planning on using our past relationship, and my trust, for the publicity and the money. He doesn't care that it would cost me my job. He was only going to do it for himself. For the money, and the publicity. There is no way I'm going to let him to destroy my life. I wonder if he even cares if he wins and I get any money at all. It's all for his image as a great lawyer."

Now she didn't want to just call Steve. She wanted him to come over so she could scratch his eyes out. Or something equally gruesome. Of course she'd never do such a thing. She would have to do the opposite—work on forgiving him, because that was what God wanted her to do. Even though it would be hard to forgive Steve, it would be worse for herself to carry the anger. It was better for everyone, including herself, if she let it go.

She would have to work on that, and work hard. Just not today. Today she was mad.

"I'd rather you simply told him you decided not to sue, not that you'd found out why."

"Why not?"

"He's a smart man. After all, he's a lawyer. If you tell him you know what he was planning, he'll figure out how you found out. We didn't actually have a conversation, but we did talk. He knew I heard the conversation, but since he thought I was a stranger, he didn't care. He'll make the connection, and I can't let that happen. I can't let him know it was me."

This was it. The time to ask the reason for all his secrecy. She sucked in a deep breath. "Why not?"

He paused, and his eyes lost focus for a few seconds.

He shifted slightly to one side and pressed one hand over the back pocket of his pants. "He said he was going to make it into a media circus, and he could still do it. I can't get involved in something like that."

He'd done it to her enough times now that she knew his pattern. She'd asked him to tell her something. In not so many words he said no, and the next thing he was going to do was to close the subject by leaving. Before he could stand and walk away, Ashley grabbed his sleeve and held on for dear life, forcing him to remain sitting. "That's not good enough. I don't understand. What have you done? Are you a secret agent or something?"

She hoped he would smile, but he didn't. Instead, his eyes glazed over for a few seconds again. "No." He shook his head. "Nothing that glamorous."

Again, she waited for him to continue. He didn't.

She released his sleeve. "Fine. Go."

Instead of leaving, he raised his hands, cupped her cheeks, and leaned closer. "I'm sorry," he muttered, then leaned forward and kissed her.

Ashley closed her eyes and kissed him back. She'd wanted this for so long, and now that it was finally happening, she didn't want it to end. She slipped her arms around him and held him tight. He made a small groan, tilted his head a little, and kissed her more firmly.

Her insides turned to butter, and her heart raced. She'd never kissed a man like this, and she didn't want to stop.

Much too soon, he pulled away. For a couple of seconds he gazed into her eyes, then slid his arms around her back and pulled her tight into a tender embrace.

She leaned into him, and hugged him back. Being locked in his arms felt better than her dreams, making her realize how long she'd wanted this. So as not to spoil the moment, she rested her head on his shoulder and enjoyed his warmth.

Until his phone rang in his pocket.

He released her, straightened, and answered it. He listened for a minute, agreed with the caller, and ended the call.

"That was my boss. I've got to go, something really important came in. He said he tried to call me earlier but he went to voice mail. I've taken so much time off lately he made it clear it's payback time. I'll be back for supper."

Before she could regain her senses they were separated and he was walking across the room. The door closed behind him, followed by the click as he locked it, and was gone.

Ashley closed her eyes to try to relive the moment. She was falling in love with him, and she couldn't let that happen. There were too many things about him she didn't know, made worse by the fact that he outright refused to tell her.

Perhaps the worst of all was saying sorry before he kissed her, when she didn't know what he was so sorry for.

Chapter 15

Dave had barely settled into his desk when his boss approached him.

Jerry dragged an empty chair to the front of his desk, and sat. "You had me worried for a while. I was ready to call Hank."

Dave couldn't even force himself to smile. "I'm okay."

"You don't look okay. Want to talk?"

Dave looked up into the face of his boss, and his most trusted ally. "I don't know what to do. It's never been this complicated before. This isn't what I signed up for. Sometimes I wish I could turn back the clock, except I know I did the right thing."

Jerry nodded. "I know. I've heard that so many times before. I want to say that it gets easier, but most of the time it doesn't. At least for you, it probably will be over in about twenty years."

Dave wanted to lower his head to the desk and groan. Or scream. Or cry. Or something. But that was too dramatic. Or maybe it wasn't. Now, more than ever, he struggled with if it was okay to wish for someone to die.

"You haven't told her, have you?"

"No. Our relationship isn't at that point. Besides, I'm not sure how she'd take it. Too many people have lied to her about hiding stuff they didn't want her to know. I don't know how she'll take it when she finds out I'm one more person with a secret life. Only with me, if something goes wrong it wouldn't be just a few days of crying over split milk. She'd be just as dead as me. I can't let her take that kind of risk."

"What if she wants to take that risk with you?"

Dave stared blankly out the window, where the bright sunshine lit up a park below. A few older people were walking little dogs, and a group of small children was playing baseball. It was a world he couldn't share.

"I can't let her take that risk."

"Why not? You're a decent guy, you've got a good job as an accountant, and you go to church on Sunday. You're a hero."

Dave pounded one fist on the desk and stared Jerry straight in the eyes. "I'm not an accountant. I'm a teacher. I may be a decent guy, but there's a price on my head. I never know if someone in the crowd has me in his sights so he can collect it. Sunday morning is the only time of the week I can relax and be myself, and not worry if some stranger in the crowd has found me. Every other minute of every other day, I'm always hiding my face and looking over my shoulder. I can't do that to her."

He let his forehead fall to the desk, and covered the back of his head with his hands. Five years ago, when he was on the witness stand telling the judge what he'd seen and heard, he wasn't a hero. He'd been a normal guy doing his civic duty. Keeping drugs off the street. Keeping the kids in his class safe.

But it hadn't ended there. The situation deteriorated, and after two attempts on his life, Dave was forced to go into witness protection.

He couldn't drag Ashley into that kind of life. Or, if they found him, that kind of death.

"I can't do this," he muttered into the desktop.

He heard the scrape of the wooden chair dragging on the floor as Jerry stood. "Do you want to take the day off? I can do this reconciliation myself. I don't mind."

Dave shook his head, his forehead still pressed into the deskpad. "No. I'm here. I need something to do."

"Want me to call Hank for you?"

He shook his head again. Unless he had a problem, he only needed to talk to his handler once a year. "No. I don't want any more counseling. I've heard enough rhetoric about making the world a better place. I want my life back."

"Sorry, bud. You did a good thing and you saved a lot of good kids by keeping many boatloads of drugs off the streets. I'll leave you alone now. I need that file by five o'clock."

Slowly, Dave righted himself, and turned on his computer. It was pointless to wish for things that couldn't be changed. He knew he'd done the right thing. His testimony had saved lives. He would have done the same thing even if he'd known at the time that it would mean giving up everything he held dear. All he could do was trust in God to continue keeping him safe.

Tonight, when he got back to Ashley's place he had to stop what was going on between them. He just wasn't sure how to do that.

He thunked his head to the desktop again.

If only he could kiss her like that one more time.

* * *

A knock sounded on the door. "It's me. Dave."

"Come in," she called.

The tinkling of his keys echoed, and the door creaked open. "I'm going to have to oil that," he muttered, looking up at the hinge. He turned to rest a very fragrant smelling bag and a bouquet of flowers on the table beside the door, pulled out his cell phone, and began tapping at it. "Just making myself a note so I don't forget."

After a few seconds he returned it to his pocket, and turned around to pick up what he'd put down.

Ashley's heart pounded. "I see what you've got. I think you spoiled the surprise."

"Surprise? It's not a surprise. I knew you'd see me when I walked in. I brought supper." Grinning, he held up a bag from her favorite Chinese food restaurant.

She grinned back. "Not the food. The flowers."

His smile dropped. "Oh. Those. What if they're not for you?"

Not only did Ashley's smile drop, so did her heart, into the bottom of her shoes. Her one shoe, anyway.

"Just kidding. Of course they're for you. I saw you had a vase in the cupboard. I'll be right back." He left the food on the coffee table, but carried the flowers with him into the kitchen.

The delicious aroma reminded her stomach that she'd skipped lunch. It made a very embarrassing grumble at exactly the same moment as Dave appeared with a vase containing the flowers in one hand, and a couple of plates and cutlery in the other.

"I'm hungry too. Dig in."

Ashley could barely contain her enthusiasm as she began to open all the containers. Dave hadn't just ordered a generic dinner for two, he'd selected all her favorites.

Her hand froze, the spoon buried in the Almond Gai Ding.

He'd brought her favorite food. He'd brought flowers.

Suddenly she lost her appetite.

She turned to him, trying to steel her heart to be ready for his answer. "Why did you do this?" As she spoke she motioned her free arm to encompass the food and flowers.

He didn't look at her as he spoke. He just kept piling food onto his plate. "I was working and didn't have time to cook, and I was hungry. I put the restaurant into my address book a couple of weeks ago." He paused and looked up. "I've got voice activated auto-dial in the car. You should try it. Bluetooth is cheaper than it's ever been."

"I don't talk on the phone in the car. I let everything go to voice mail and check it when I stop the car."

"So you're an old-fashioned kind of girl. That's nice." He paused, then sat back with his plate. "Isn't that an oxymoron? An old-fashioned girl with a cell phone. Just what defines old-fashioned anymore? Cell phones have been around for over twenty years in various forms and technologies, so that does make them old in a way, but when I think of old-fashioned and phones, I think of those big, black rotary-dial models. Do you know most kids don't even know what a rotary dial phone looks like? And when you say the phone rings, when is the last time a phone with a real bell ringer was even available? It's all been electronic ringtones for at least a decade."

"You're babbling. What is it you don't want to tell me?" Of course, she'd learned the hard way there were many things he didn't want to tell her. Now there was apparently one more to add to the list.

His eyes widened. "Why do you ask that?"

Ashley's eyes narrowed. "Why are you answering a question with a question?"

"Busted." He lowered his plate to his lap. "Did you call Steve this afternoon?"

"Yes." She doubted the special treatment was to make her feel better about telling what she thought of Steve without getting specific on his devious attempt to get her involved in a court case. "It was hard not to tell him what a jerk he was about the court case without going into the reasons, but I still told him I thought he was a jerk in general." She smiled. "It felt really good."

"Good."

She waited for him to comment further. All he did was sip his tea.

"What is it you don't want to tell me?" Not that he would give her a list, but he probably could.

A thick pause hung between them until finally he answered. "I think it's best if we stayed just friends. There are some things I need to think about, and I need space."

This time she really lost her appetite. "Does that mean this is goodbye?"

He shook his head. "No. I still want to help you with everything while you're laid up. I meant exactly what I said. I want to be just friends. Like, no benefits or stuff like that." He set his plate down on the coffee table, and moved to sit beside her. Slowly, he lifted her plate from her numb fingers, also set it on the table, and clasped both her hands in his. "We can be friends, can't we?"

Dazed, she looked into his eyes, down to his mouth, then back to his eyes. His pupils were dilated, even in the bright light, his full lips slightly parted.

He wanted to kiss her. She knew he did. She wanted to kiss him, too.

But friends didn't kiss. Friends were…just friends.

She cleared her throat, but still her voice didn't come out like normal. "Sure. Friends. We can do that."

He dropped her hands, sat back, and reached for the remote with one hand and his plate with the other. "Good. I think *MythBusters* is on. Let's watch it."

Chapter 16

Dave checked his watch for probably the twentieth time. He pressed his hand to his pocket, feeling the bump that was his phone. He'd promised he'd call Evan with an update. If only he had one to give.

Any minute, Ashley would come hobbling out of the doctor's office, only this time it wouldn't be with crutches, but with a cane.

Today was the day the cast was scheduled to come off. Unless something had gone horribly wrong and no one noticed.

He didn't want to hope that she would need the cast for another few weeks, yet he did. That would give him an excuse to stick around.

Since the day he'd told her they needed to be just friends, that was exactly what happened. If he hadn't already been enough in love with her then, whatever had blossomed between them morphed into something that he'd only read about in books. They were more than friends. They were soul mates. They enjoyed the same books. They loved the same television shows. They both found the same things funny, and became angry at the same situations.

She'd even made him watch the goose movie again, and he'd sniffled like an idiot right alongside her.

He didn't want to give that up.

He'd sacrificed everything in his life. His home, his friends, his family, his career. He couldn't give up Ashley, too.

It was a mixed feeling of joy and terror he felt when Ashley hobbled into the lobby, a painful grin on her face, a cane in her hand, and the doctor behind, carrying the crutches.

Dave jumped to his feet and hustled over to her. "How are you? How does it feel? Do you feel shaky? Faint? Do you need help?"

The doctor grinned, handed the crutches to Dave, then turned and walked away without commenting.

"I'm fine. Considering. Come on, I want to go. Just not home. I want to go somewhere I'll need to bend my knee. Because I finally can."

"Okay. Just remember not to overdo it. This isn't going to be instantaneous. It's still going to be a while before you can walk without stiffness, and even longer to walk unaided."

She grinned at him. His heart fluttered in his chest. "Funny, I just heard all that exact same stuff a minute ago. Thank you, Dr. Dave."

"I remember what it was like, that's all," he muttered, trying to sound grumpy. But instead of feeling grumpy, he felt scared. Not the usual kind of scared, a different kind.

He was terrified this was the end. She was doing fine,

so he had no more excuse to spend every spare minute with her, or even a few minutes that weren't spare.

He gulped. "I'll go anywhere you want."

They continued slowly to the elevator. Once inside she raised one hand above the panel, and let it hover. "Isn't this where one of us hits the button to stop the elevator between floors and we talk about something really important that we can't let anyone else hear?"

"Maybe." He probably should have grinned, but he couldn't.

"This is going to sound strange, but I changed my mind. I want to go home. I want to get Chinese food and eat in the kitchen, at the table, with my leg bent. We can make that tea you like so much, and just relax. With my knee bent."

"Okay." He noticed she'd said the part about bending her knee twice. He remembered what that felt like, so he didn't say anything.

Small talk had never been so painful. By the time they made it to her kitchen their conversation had dwindled into silence, and he felt like he'd been pulled through a wringer. Twice.

Ashley maneuvered herself into a chair while he put the kettle on to make the tea.

As he turned around, she looked up at him. "Why does this feel so awkward?"

Dave's stomach churned. He hadn't been hungry before, and now that they were in the kitchen he felt like he needed to vomit more than he needed to eat. "Because this should be the point where I had planned to say you're going to be fine, and we go our separate ways."

"You don't need to do that. I've honored your request not to ask you any questions about it since you asked me not to, but I think we've passed that point. I know the person you are. I don't think there's anything you could have done that would change that."

Dave gulped. "Yeah. There is."

"Please. Sit down."

He dragged the chair beside her, sat, and grasped her hands. But his vocal cords wouldn't work.

She looked at him, eye to eye since they were both seated. "Do you trust me? The answer is yes or no. If it's yes, then you can tell me." She stopped, swallowed, and her eyes began to get glassy, tearing up. She cleared her throat, and her voice came out sounding almost strangled. "If it's no, then get up and leave, and we'll never see each other again."

That was pretty blunt, and she was right. It did come down to trust, and this really was a yes or no answer.

In only ten short weeks, he'd fallen totally and completely in love with Ashley. He wanted to tell her so. If she loved him, that was the time for her to say she loved him back, except he hadn't given her the complete picture of who he was. Before she could love him back, she needed to know the truth.

He clasped her hands tighter. "I trust you. What I'm going to tell you is something you can never, ever tell anyone, ever. Only a few people know, and it's got to stay that way. Even if you never want to see me again, I'm going to trust that you will never tell this to anyone, no matter what."

One side of her mouth quivered. "You're making this sound like CSI Los Angeles. You told me you weren't a secret agent."

"I'm far from a secret agent." He cleared his throat, and looked down at their joined hands. "Here goes. Are you ready?"

"Yes."

"Before I was an accountant, I was a high school math teacher. A bunch of my students were on a community ball team and one Saturday they invited me to watch. While I was there one of the boy's sisters lost her little dog, so I left the game to help look for it. The dog ended up going into the community center building. It was a real small dog, and somehow it got into one of the storage closets."

"How did you find it?"

"The leash was trailing, I saw a bit of it sticking out. I got the key from the maintenance guy and went in to get the dog. Its hair had gotten tangled up on a broken metal shelf that had collapsed. While I was trying to get the dog free the door closed behind me, but I didn't care, I had a key, I wasn't locked in or anything. It was dark, so I got my cell phone out of my pocket and used it for light, and then I heard voices. They started talking about a shipment of drugs coming in. It wasn't just a drug deal. This was big-time trafficking. Heroin. They were talking shipyard."

Dave paused to let the magnitude of what he was saying sink in.

"What did you do?"

"I stayed really, really quiet. I was all alone, locked in a closet with a potentially yappy dog. Fortunately she didn't bark. I didn't know if I should pick her up at that point, so I didn't. As a teacher I saw some drug abuse with a few of the students, so that's always a major issue with me. But these weren't students, they were parents. One of them was the parent of one of my students. Since I had my phone in my hand I took a video of the conversation through the vent, which included stealing a car and extortion as well as the drug import. This was a big-time gang deal. I got almost the whole conversation."

Ashley gasped. "Weren't you scared?"

"More scared than I'd ever been in my life. Up to that point, anyway. When they left I found a knife and cut the dog's hair to get it free, gave her to the little girl, and went straight to the police. With what I gave them, they made a huge drug bust, arrested dozens of people, and pretty much shut down the cartel. There was a lot of jail time sentenced for a lot of people over that."

"Then that's good. Isn't it?"

He nodded. "Yes, but not everyone got arrested. The other man on the video was the cartel leader, who got a lot of jail time. He might never see the light of day outside prison walls. One that didn't get arrested was his son due to lack of evidence. With his family in jail and his source of income yanked out from under him, he was not a happy guy. A few days after the trial was over I had just got to the bank and he came up behind me at the ATM. At first I didn't recognize him, but he was fidgety and making me really nervous. When there was only one person in line ahead of me I turned around and recognized him. Instead of going to the machine, I stepped out of the line and left really fast. He didn't go to the machine either. He busted out of the line, and I ran. Execution style, he raised his gun and fired at me as I was running through the parking lot."

Ashley pulled her hands out of his, pressed them to her mouth, and gasped.

"If you've heard enough, I'll stop."

"Don't stop. Did he hit you?"

Dave pressed one hand to his shoulder. "Yup. It still hurts when the weather changes."

"Did they catch him?"

Dave made a wry smile. "You know that saying that there's never a cop around when you need one? It's not true. One of the customers who was standing in line at the bank was a cop on his lunch break. He ran out when the shots started firing and took him down." He closed his eyes, and sucked in a deep breath. "I'll never forget what that felt like, running for my life with a gun pointed at me. I dove behind a car. That's probably why he didn't hit any vital organs."

"That's how you know what it's like to be shot. How horrible!"

"That's not the end. Remember, this wasn't small-time. This was a huge cartel, and my testimony was the last link that took down the whole organization, locally anyway. After both the father with all the higher-ups and then the son got arrested I thought I would be okay. I was driving through the park one day when out of the corner of my eye I saw a guy in the car beside me pointing a gun at me. I'd already been shot once, so I didn't give this a lot of thought. The line I was in was barely moving, which left me a sitting duck. I undid my seat belt and scrambled out of the car, but in the middle of a bridge I had nowhere to go. This was just a park, so they didn't have high side railings. I wasn't going to run the length of the bridge with a guy pointing a gun at me, so I ran through traffic to the other side and jumped over the railing and into the water. It turns out the water wasn't very deep, and that's how I broke my leg."

She sat there in silence, staring at him like he'd grown another head.

"That time was a targeted hit. There's a contract out on me, confirmed by an informant, which they figure will last until both the father and son die. So they faked my death, I had some plastic surgery, lost forty pounds, and they changed my name, moved me across the country, and put me into witness protection."

He stopped, waiting for her to say something.

After a minute or so of silence, Dave stood. "I think it's time for me to go. If you can live with that, you know where to find me."

Ashley heard the door close, but she couldn't get up. Not that her legs couldn't move—they just wouldn't.

Of all the reasons she'd imagined for his secrecy, and there had been many, this hadn't been one of them. She wasn't even close.

Witness protection. Now she knew why he dyed his hair and wore that ball cap all the time. That was also why he hid from all cameras and didn't go out much in public places.

She tried to think of this in practical terms, but it was so far out of her realm of experience she didn't know where to start.

The only thing she could think of was to phone Tasha.

Her fingers shook as she hit the buttons on her cell phone. The longer it took Tasha to pick up, the harder she clenched her teeth with every ring.

"Hi, Tasha, it's me. Ashley. I need to talk to you. Have you got a minute?"

"Sure. What about?"

"It's about Dave. I know what it is he's been hiding from me."

"It's about time. How did you find out?"

"He told me." Now that he had, she could understand why it was so hard for him, and why it took so long. The level of trust had to be one hundred percent.

"Is it bad?"

She opened her mouth, but no answer came out. In a personal sense, it wasn't bad in the way her father had cheated on her mother, or in the way that Steve had been ready to throw her to the media like taking a lamb to the slaughter. It was worse, because a modern-day version of the mob had a hit out on him, and that was very bad. But she couldn't tell her friend he was in witness protection. That would compromise his safety. "I can't say."

"What did he do?"

Again she opened her mouth, then she snapped it shut. Everything that happened had either been in the courts, in the news, or in the public eye. It all was public record, but he couldn't in any way be linked to a single event because being identified could mean his death in the wrong hands. "I can't say."

"Was it legal?"

That she could answer. He'd testified in court to do the right thing to stop the flow of illegal drugs, and to put the bad guys in jail. "Yes."

"Okay... Is it really such a big secret?"

The biggest. Exposing him could mean his death. As she nearly said that, she snapped her mouth shut. Talking on a cell phone was a huge lack of security. A few times she'd heard her neighbor's cell phone conversation on the wireless speakers for her television. She certainly couldn't say anything over the cell phone that could compromise Dave's safety. "Yes."

"This is crazy. You phone to talk, and you haven't really told me anything. Is this an item of national security or something?"

That answer, she knew. It was yes. Which she couldn't say. But she couldn't say that she couldn't say, because if someone were listening, anything other than a no would be taken as a yes.

"Ashley? Are you there? What's going on?"

Even in one short conversation, she was beginning to understand what Dave had to go through, every minute of every day of his life. He'd done this for the safety of people he didn't even know, just because it was the right thing to do.

Not only was he her own personal hero, he was the hero of hundreds if not thousands of people, and they didn't even know his name.

"I'm here. What's going on is that I'm in love with Dave. It was great talking to you. I've got to go."

Chapter 17

Since he didn't have a couch, Dave sat on the small mattress on the floor that had been his bed for the last few months and stared blankly at the wall.

His renter had already moved out a couple of weeks ago, so all he had to do was pack up what little he'd brought, donate the few pieces of furniture he'd bought to Goodwill, and he was free to go back to his real home, as much as he could call it home. He was ready to leave there with only a few minutes' notice, too.

Such was what his life had to be.

He couldn't blame Ashley for not wanting to get involved with him. If it were the other way around, he probably would have felt the same way. Hindsight was a wonderful thing, and now he was wishing he hadn't told her. Even though there was always something missing, at least they had a relationship. He'd never spent time with anyone and been so happy, even before the ugliness that changed his life.

If only he could take back his words. The shock on her face told him everything he needed to know, and when she didn't try to stop him as he left, that confirmed it. He couldn't blame her for not wanting to get involved with him. The reality of what his life had become would scare any sane person away, especially someone so pure and full of life as Ashley.

Except for not telling her about what he'd been five years ago, she was the only person who knew him as he really was, and she liked him anyway.

After he was gone from her life, he had no doubt that she would keep his secret. She was honorable and fair, and everything he could have wanted in a life partner, if that were even possible anymore.

Obviously it wasn't.

He swiped his hands over his eyes, then got up to blow his nose. Everyone left home at some point, some further than others. Lots of people never went back. The difference with him was that he had no choice. It was painful, but not unbearable.

Having to be separated from Ashley, on the other hand, felt like he'd been ripped in two.

Since he was alone, and he was going to stay that way, while he was behind closed doors he took out his contacts and put his glasses on, then looked at himself in the mirror. If he'd learned anything from Ashley, this was a good time to watch the goose movie, and he could, because she had an extra copy and had given it to him.

He returned to the living room, picked up the remote, dragged the mattress into the living room, tossed the large pillow he'd bought against the wall, plopped down on his makeshift couch, and aimed the remote at the television.

Just as he hit the button, banging came from the door.

He froze and broke out into a cold sweat.

"Dave?" Ashley's voice echoed through the door. "It's me. Ashley. Can I come in?"

At first he relaxed, then he stiffened and looked to the bathroom. He needed to put his contacts back in. But then again, she already knew everything there was to know. She could see him as he really was, and it wouldn't matter.

He stood, walked to the door, and opened it.

"I want to…" her voice trailed off. "You're wearing glasses."

"Would you like to come in?" he asked and stood back for her to enter.

Using the cane, she hobbled in, then stood in the middle of his nearly bare living room.

"I'd offer you a seat, but I don't really have one. I can bring you the chair from the desk I have in the bedroom."

At he said "bedroom" her head turned toward the mattress on the floor.

"It doubles as a couch during the daytime."

"Have you been living like this for the past ten weeks?"

He shrugged. "I haven't spent much time here. It's been adequate."

She turned back to his face. "You have beautiful eyes. They're blue."

"I normally wear colored contacts."

"But your driver's license said your eyes are brown, and it didn't say anything about corrective lenses."

He shrugged his shoulders again. "I know. It's part of the cover. You probably already know I dye my hair, too. It's really a lot lighter than this." He ran his fingers through his dark brown hair. "It's probably time for me to touch up the roots again."

She wobbled a bit, leaning on the cane. "Can we sit down? I don't mind sitting on the mattress. I'll just need help getting up again."

It was rather embarrassing, but it really didn't matter. He had nothing left to lose.

Once they were settled she turned to him. "Tell me about the real Dave Ducharme. That isn't your real name, is it?"

"No. My real name is Dale Bellamy. They said it's important for the new first name to start the same way as the old one. That's so it's easier to respond automatically when people call me by the wrong name."

"Would you like me to call you Dale?"

"No. I'm Dave now. Dale Bellamy is dead." He reached into his back pocket and pulled a couple of photos out of his wallet. First he handed her the photo of his cemetery marker. "This is my gravestone. They staged a car accident in which I died. Which was too bad. I had a really nice car. They had a funeral for me and everything. The only ones who know I'm not really dead are my parents and my sister." He squeezed his eyes shut. "I hated to do that to my students. My mother told me all about my funeral. Half the school was there. There were photos of me everywhere, and I got a great memorial write-up in the yearbook that year."

Her eyes widened. "Did you leave anyone else behind? Like a girlfriend?"

He shook his head. "No. Nothing serious."

"Why do you carry this with you?"

"Every time I get frustrated, I pull this out as a reminder of what could happen if I let myself get sloppy. It's not far-fetched. They almost succeeded twice."

"Let me see the one of your family." He started to choke up as he handed her the photo, the only one he had of his past. "My parents, and my sister, Lisa. It's too risky to email them, but a couple of times a year we exchange birthday cards and letters through my handler, Hank. To them, I'm Uncle Joe from Canada. They sign their real names to me."

"How can you do this?"

"A better question would be, how could I not? It's not like I can turn back time or tell the courts I take it back. It's done, and I have to live with it. I helped put a dent in the drug trade for a while, and that's got to be good enough."

"Since you went into witness protection, have you ever had to pack up and run?"

"No. As you can see, I'm very careful with where I go and when. It's kind of lonely, but for the most part, I'm safe."

He pulled the last picture out of his wallet. "This is the real me, the old Dale Bellamy."

As Ashley gasped at the old photo, her mouth literally dropped open. "This doesn't even look like you. At all."

Besides the glasses, blue eyes, and blond-brown hair, I shaved off the beard. Plus I've had a nose job and I lost forty pounds."

"Is that why you were so obsessive with our diets?"

He felt his cheeks heat up. "Yeah. I really struggle to keep it off. I don't think most men appreciate how much work it can be, but I do. I have to keep up the exercise twice a week, and at my real apartment building, there's a fully equipped exercise room. I use it a lot."

"How many people know? Besides me."

He counted on his fingers. My handler, Hank. My

boss, Jerry. They kind of work together. He's had other people in witness protection programs work for him. He's a great guy, and gives me a lot of leeway. Then there's my best friend Tyler and now his wife, Brittany. My pastor, Rob. I told your boss, Principal Bev, a little, but only as much as she needed to know for me to do the job for two days. And now you. That's it."

She reached over and grasped both his hands. "That's not many. Do you think you'll ever get married?"

"I hadn't thought about it that much until Tyler got married. I'd like to, but I don't think it's ever going to happen. It's asking too much for someone to live like that, to be prepared to leave everyone and everything on a potential minute's notice. Everything I value, I keep in one box, ready to grab and run if I need to. I couldn't do that to someone."

She squeezed his hands. "You could do that to me. I wouldn't mind."

Dave's heart started to pound in his chest. "Really? You'd marry me?"

She released his hands, then reached up to rest her palm on his cheek. "Yes. I'll marry you. In fact, I'll marry you as soon as I can walk again without the cane."

His throat tightened, and he struggled to breathe. If he was understanding this correctly, she'd taken his question as a proposal, and accepted. "Really?" If so, she'd just made him the happiest man on earth.

She nodded. "Really. Under one condition."

Before she could name the condition, just in case he couldn't do it, he turned, wrapped his arms around her, and kissed her with all the love in his heart. When she kissed him back the same way, he wondered if he needed to pinch himself to make sure it was really happening.

But he had to know. He pulled away, just enough so his lips brushed hers as he spoke. "What's the condition?"

He felt her smile more than he saw it. "That from now on, we do all our banking online."

He smiled back. "Consider it done."

* * * * *

REQUEST YOUR FREE BOOKS!

2 FREE INSPIRATIONAL NOVELS
PLUS 2
FREE
MYSTERY GIFTS

Love Inspired®

YES! Please send me 2 FREE Love Inspired® novels and my 2 FREE mystery gifts (gifts are worth about $10). After receiving them, if I don't wish to receive any more books, I can return the shipping statement marked "cancel." If I don't cancel, I will receive 6 brand-new novels every month and be billed just $4.74 per book in the U.S. or $5.24 per book in Canada. That's a savings of at least 21% off the cover price. It's quite a bargain! Shipping and handling is just 50¢ per book in the U.S. and 75¢ per book in Canada.* I understand that accepting the 2 free books and gifts places me under no obligation to buy anything. I can always return a shipment and cancel at any time. Even if I never buy another book, the two free books and gifts are mine to keep forever.

105/305 IDN F49N

Name	(PLEASE PRINT)	

Address		Apt. #

City	State/Prov.	Zip/Postal Code

Signature (if under 18, a parent or guardian must sign)

Mail to the Harlequin® Reader Service:
IN U.S.A.: P.O. Box 1867, Buffalo, NY 14240-1867
IN CANADA: P.O. Box 609, Fort Erie, Ontario L2A 5X3

**Are you a subscriber to Love Inspired books
and want to receive the larger-print edition?
Call 1-800-873-8635 or visit www.ReaderService.com.**

* Terms and prices subject to change without notice. Prices do not include applicable taxes. Sales tax applicable in N.Y. Canadian residents will be charged applicable taxes. Offer not valid in Quebec. This offer is limited to one order per household. Not valid for current subscribers to Love Inspired books. All orders subject to credit approval. Credit or debit balances in a customer's account(s) may be offset by any other outstanding balance owed by or to the customer. Please allow 4 to 6 weeks for delivery. Offer available while quantities last.

Your Privacy—The Harlequin® Reader Service is committed to protecting your privacy. Our Privacy Policy is available online at www.ReaderService.com or upon request from the Harlequin Reader Service.
We make a portion of our mailing list available to reputable third parties that offer products we believe may interest you. If you prefer that we not exchange your name with third parties, or if you wish to clarify or modify your communication preferences, please visit us at www.ReaderService.com/consumerschoice or write to us at Harlequin Reader Service Preference Service, P.O. Box 9062, Buffalo, NY 14269. Include your complete name and address.

LIDIR13R

REQUEST YOUR FREE BOOKS!

2 FREE INSPIRATIONAL NOVELS
PLUS 2
FREE
MYSTERY GIFTS

Love Inspired
HISTORICAL
INSPIRATIONAL HISTORICAL ROMANCE

YES! Please send me 2 FREE Love Inspired® Historical novels and my 2 FREE mystery gifts (gifts are worth about $10). After receiving them, if I don't wish to receive any more books, I can return the shipping statement marked "cancel." If I don't cancel, I will receive 4 brand-new novels every month and be billed just $4.74 per book in the U.S. or $5.24 per book in Canada. That's a savings of at least 21% off the cover price. It's quite a bargain! Shipping and handling is just 50¢ per book in the U.S. and 75¢ per book in Canada.* I understand that accepting the 2 free books and gifts places me under no obligation to buy anything. I can always return a shipment and cancel at any time. Even if I never buy another book, the two free books and gifts are mine to keep forever.

102/302 IDN F5CY

Name	(PLEASE PRINT)
Address	Apt. #
City	State/Prov.	Zip/Postal Code

Signature (if under 18, a parent or guardian must sign)

Mail to the Harlequin® Reader Service:
IN U.S.A.: P.O. Box 1867, Buffalo, NY 14240-1867
IN CANADA: P.O. Box 609, Fort Erie, Ontario L2A 5X3

Want to try two free books from another series?
Call 1-800-873-8635 or visit www.ReaderService.com.

* Terms and prices subject to change without notice. Prices do not include applicable taxes. Sales tax applicable in N.Y. Canadian residents will be charged applicable taxes. Offer not valid in Quebec. This offer is limited to one order per household. Not valid for current subscribers to Love Inspired Historical books. All orders subject to credit approval. Credit or debit balances in a customer's account(s) may be offset by any other outstanding balance owed by or to the customer. Please allow 4 to 6 weeks for delivery. Offer available while quantities last.

Your Privacy—The Harlequin® Reader Service is committed to protecting your privacy. Our Privacy Policy is available online at www.ReaderService.com or upon request from the Harlequin Reader Service.

We make a portion of our mailing list available to reputable third parties that offer products we believe may interest you. If you prefer that we not exchange your name with third parties, or if you wish to clarify or modify your communication preferences, please visit us at www.ReaderService.com/consumerchoice or write to us at Harlequin Reader Service Preference Service, P.O. Box 9062, Buffalo, NY 14269. Include your complete name and address.

LIHDIR13R

REQUEST YOUR FREE BOOKS!
2 FREE WHOLESOME ROMANCE NOVELS IN LARGER PRINT
PLUS 2
FREE
MYSTERY GIFTS

✻✻✻✻✻✻✻✻✻✻✻✻✻✻✻✻✻✻✻✻✻✻✻✻

HEARTWARMING™

❀❀❀❀❀❀❀❀❀❀❀❀❀❀❀❀❀❀❀❀❀❀

Wholesome, tender romances

YES! Please send me 2 FREE Harlequin® Heartwarming Larger-Print novels and my 2 FREE mystery gifts (gifts worth about $10). After receiving them, if I don't wish to receive any more books, I can return the shipping statement marked "cancel." If I don't cancel, I will receive 4 brand-new larger-print novels every month and be billed just $4.99 per book in the U.S. or $5.74 per book in Canada. That's a savings of at least 23% off the cover price. It's quite a bargain! Shipping and handling is just 50¢ per book in the U.S. and 75¢ per book in Canada.* I understand that accepting the 2 free books and gifts places me under no obligation to buy anything. I can always return a shipment and cancel at any time. Even if I never buy another book, the two free books and gifts are mine to keep forever.

161/361 IDN F47N

Name _____ (PLEASE PRINT) _____

Address _____ Apt. #

City _____ State/Prov. _____ Zip/Postal Code

Signature (if under 18, a parent or guardian must sign)

Mail to the **Harlequin® Reader Service:**
IN U.S.A.: P.O. Box 1867, Buffalo, NY 14240-1867
IN CANADA: P.O. Box 609, Fort Erie, Ontario L2A 5X3

* Terms and prices subject to change without notice. Prices do not include applicable taxes. Sales tax applicable in N.Y. Canadian residents will be charged applicable taxes. Offer not valid in Quebec. This offer is limited to one order per household. Not valid for current subscribers to Harlequin Heartwarming larger-print books. All orders subject to credit approval. Credit or debit balances in a customer's account(s) may be offset by any other outstanding balance owed by or to the customer. Please allow 4 to 6 weeks for delivery. Offer available while quantities last.

Your Privacy—The Harlequin® Reader Service is committed to protecting your privacy. Our Privacy Policy is available online at www.ReaderService.com or upon request from the Harlequin Reader Service.

We make a portion of our mailing list available to reputable third parties that offer products we believe may interest you. If you prefer that we not exchange your name with third parties, or if you wish to clarify or modify your communication preferences, please visit us at www.ReaderService.com/consumerchoice or write to us at Harlequin Reader Service Preference Service, P.O. Box 9062, Buffalo, NY 14269. Include your complete name and address.

HWDIR13R